#1
5.50
D
9/80

DESIGNS ON LIFE

By E. X. Ferrars

DESIGNS ON LIFE

E. X. FERRARS

PUBLISHED FOR THE CRIME CLUB BY
DOUBLEDAY & COMPANY, INC.
GARDEN CITY, NEW YORK
1980

ISBN: 0-385-15770-3
Library of Congress Catalog Card Number 79-8283
Copyright © 1980 by M. D. Brown
All Rights Reserved
Printed in the United States of America
First Edition

Acknowledgements

"After Death the Deluge" by E. X. Ferrars. Originally published by Faber in 1940. Copyright © 1940 by M. D. Brown. Reprinted by permission of the author.

"The Truthful Witness" by E. X. Ferrars. Originally published in the *Crime Writers Association Anthology* in 1958. Copyright © 1959 by M. D. Brown. Reprinted by permission of the author.

"Go, Lovely Rose" by E. X. Ferrars. Originally published in the August 1976 issue of *Ellery Queen's Mystery Magazine*. Copyright © 1976 by M. D. Brown. Reprinted by permission of the author.

"Drawn into Error" by E. X. Ferrars. Originally published in the December 1957 issue of *Alfred Hitchcock Mystery Magazine*. Copyright © 1957 by M. D. Brown. Reprinted by permission of the author.

"Safety" by E. X. Ferrars. Originally published in the July 1958 issue of *Suspense*. Copyright © 1958 by M. D. Brown. Reprinted by permission of the author.

"A Very Small Thing" by E. X. Ferrars. Originally published in the August 1959 issue of *Ellery Queen's Mystery Magazine*. Copyright © 1959 by M. D. Brown. Reprinted by permission of the author.

"Scatter His Ashes" by E. X. Ferrars. Originally published in the 1970 edition of *Macmillan Winter Crimes*. Copyright © 1970 by M. D. Brown. Reprinted by permission of the author.

"Undue Influence" by E. X. Ferrars. Originally published in the 1974 edition of *Macmillan Winter Crimes*. Copyright © 1974 by M. D. Brown. Reprinted by permission of the author.

Ferrars

CONTENTS

DESIGNS ON LIFE

THE DREADFUL BELL

Helen Benson had known what the stairs would be like. She knew those old Edinburgh houses. She had spent her childhood in one of them. But what she had not realised was that the furnished flat that Colin had rented for them while she was in hospital was on the top floor.

He told her that only when they were on their way through the town in a taxi from the airport. He had met her there and had helped her out of the wheelchair that the air-line had laid on for her and into the taxi and they were already past the suburbs and entering the region of tall, formidable, dark stone houses before he mentioned that she would have three flights of stairs to climb.

"*Three* flights?" she said in a startled, disbelieving voice. "But, Colin, I can't! How can I get this thing up *three* flights of stairs?"

She used one of her sticks to hit the plaster on her leg.

He looked apologetic and distraught, a look that always made it difficult for her to hold anything against him for long. It frequently appeared on his face when he was compelled to deal with anything practical.

"But honestly I couldn't find anything else," he said, "and the rent's so low and it's really quite pleasant when you get there. I'm sure you're going to like it. The thing is to take the stairs slowly. You'll manage all right."

"I'll have to, shan't I?"

She looked out of the taxi window. There had been a powdering of snow in the night, which had turned to dirty slush on the pavements. A sky of tarnished grey hung low above the rooftops, promising more snow. After five years in one of the small, new African countries where the sun shone every day and flowers bloomed all the year round, it felt bitterly cold.

"I did my best," Colin said unhappily.

"I'm sure you did." She patted his hand. He was wearing his defensive face now, which made him look as if he were preparing to be deeply, unjustifiably hurt, but bravely to put up with it. Only the trouble was that he never did put up with it bravely when he was hurt. He could lose his temper in a flash and be far more deadly than Helen ever was to him. Or that was how she saw it herself, perhaps mistakenly. But the last thing that she wanted at the moment, when they were trying so hard to make a new beginning, was one of their scenes. She had enough to put up with without that.

The taxi turned into a street that she remembered from her childhood, though she did not think that she had ever been into any of the houses. They were tall and stark, with two centuries of grime upon them, yet with a good deal of dignity, although the street, which might once have been considered a fine one, now had a depressing air of decay. There was a seedy-looking tobacconist at one corner, opposite a greengrocer, whose goods, outside his window, spilled out of their boxes on to the pavement. The stone steps up to the doorways were worn and looked slimy with the morning's slush. As the taxi stopped at one of the houses the first big, damp flakes of a new snow-fall drifted waveringly down.

Colin jumped quickly out of the taxi, paid the driver and turned to lift Helen's two suitcases out of it. Then he reached up to help her down. She gritted her teeth at the pain as she moved. He handed her her two sticks to support her weight as she stood on the pavement, where he left her for a moment while he carried her luggage into the house. She realised that the effect of the pills that she had taken before she started on the journey had worn off. She would take two more as soon as she reached the flat, but first, she had those three flights of stairs to face. She felt a little dizzy when she thought of them, wondering if in fact there was any possibility that she would be able to climb them.

But what would she do if she could not? The taxi was already moving off. It was too late to call it back and say that she wanted to be taken to a hotel, one with a lift and no stairs to trouble her. And the snow was coming down faster. There was nothing for it but to try to reach the flat.

The stairs were just as she had imagined them, bleak stone worn hollow by two hundred years of footsteps. The house was of a type common in Edinburgh, with the two lower storeys a self-contained dwelling with an entrance of its own, and with these stairs mounting at the side of it to the flat above, without any doors opening on to any of the landings where the stairs turned back on themselves. Each flight was long, because all the rooms in the lower house were very high. There was a cold iron handrail.

Colin left the suitcases at the foot of the stairs, put an arm round Helen's waist, and while she put an arm round his shoulders, took most of her weight as she hobbled from step to step. After every few of them she paused to draw a shuddering breath, trying to pretend that it was not hurting as much as it was.

"Once I get to the top I'll never be able to come down again," she said as they reached the first landing.

"You won't need to," he said. "I'll see to everything. Just take it slowly. You're doing fine. And really, you'll like it when you get there."

She knew that that was possible. When this house had been built, staircases like this were regarded as part of the street and were most of them bare and unlovely. But often the flats opening off them had rooms of the greatest magnificence, with nobly lofty ceilings, finely proportioned windows and Adam fireplaces. She tried to hope for the best, and somehow, after she did not know how long, reached the top landing.

There were evidently two flats there, for there were two doors, side by side. Colin let go of Helen to feel for the key in his pocket. As he did so, one of the doors opened a few inches, as far as the chain holding it would allow, and singularly blue eyes in an aged, wrinkled face peered out at them. Red hair in a tangle hung over the lined forehead. A thin hand held the collar of a green quilted dressing-gown close up to the withered neck.

"You won't ring the bell, will you?" the old woman said abruptly. "If you ring it, she comes, but she doesn't like it. Remember that."

The door closed.

Helen looked at Colin in astonishment. "What was that?"

"Just a lonely old body, gone a little peculiar," he said. "She's quite harmless. In fact, she's been very kind to me since I moved in last week."

"But why should we ring the bell? There's no one to answer it."

"Why indeed?" He fitted the key into the lock and opened the door. "Now just a little further," he said. "Then you can sit down and be comfortable and I'll bring you a drink."

"What about my luggage?"

"I'll get that in a minute."

He helped her forward into the flat.

Except for the smell of dry rot that was wafted to her as soon as she entered it, it was more or less as she had expected. There was a spacious hall, with an elegant archway halfway along it and a polished floor of thick, broad old boards with a narrow runner of red carpet up the middle of it. Several doors opened off the hall, immensely solid-looking. Colin pushed one of them open and led Helen into a big room with two tall sash windows, a high ceiling with a cornice of delicately moulded plaster and a fine marble chimney-piece.

There was no fire in the old black basket grate, but an electric fire stood on the hearth in front of it, with three bars alight, and in spite of the snow now beginning to swirl thickly against the window-panes, the room felt pleasantly warm.

"I turned the fire on before I went out to meet you, so that it'd be nice when you got here," Colin said, "but actually the place is surprisingly easy to heat. The walls are about a yard thick and once you've managed to warm things up inside, they keep it in."

Helen took off her coat and lowered herself into a chair beside the fireplace.

"That old woman next door," she said. "Are we going to have trouble with her?"

"I told you, she's just mildly eccentric," he said. "Actually she's helped me quite a bit. She told me where the best shops are locally and advised me about getting in supplies, and when she knew you were coming she brought round a chicken casserole that we've only got to warm up when we want it. Now I'll go and get your things. I shan't be a moment."

He went out, closing the door behind him to keep the warmth in the room.

Helen leant back in her chair and looked round her, taking in the room with its curious mixture of grandeur and decay. Once, she thought, it must have been beautiful. It would have been a fine background for elegantly dressed ladies with hoops and powdered hair and patches. But in those days it would not have been filled with shabby Victorian furniture, sufficiently comfort-

able and not positively ugly, but without any particular character. It would not have had that faint, pervasive smell of mildew.
Other smells, perhaps, even more disagreeable, for the sanitation
would have been primitive, but that would have been normal
and would have gone unnoticed. Exhausted by her climb up the
stairs, she closed her eyes for a moment, then, opening them,
suddenly noticed the bell beside the fireplace.

It was the kind of bell that consists of a circle of painted
china, with a handle at the side of it, with a small china knob
that would have to be pulled downwards to set wires jangling
and bells ringing in the kitchen. The bell was white and its dec-
oration was a pretty little wreath of rosebuds. It was a dainty,
charming object, but it had probably not been in use for fifty
years. On an impulse, Helen reached out and pulled the handle.

There was only silence. No bell rang. The wires that the handle had once set working, had no doubt been broken long ago.

Opening her handbag, she took out the bottle with her pills in
it and swallowed two, then closed her eyes again. The pills took
some time to work. It would be at least half an hour before they
began to give her any relief from pain, but meanwhile it would
be pleasant to doze. But suddenly she became aware of a
draught on the back of her neck, a very chill draught, and looking round to see where it was coming from, she saw that the
heavy door, which she remembered Colin had closed, was standing open.

He reappeared in the room a moment later, carrying the suitcases. He closed the door. Then, after one look at Helen, he
asked quickly, "What's the matter?"

"Nothing," she said.

"Is the pain bad?"

"Just about average. I've just taken my pills. They'll help
soon."

"But you look as if—I don't know what—something had happened to you."

She gave an uncertain laugh. "It's just silly. I don't know why, but I suddenly took it into my head to ring that bell there, and of course it's broken and doesn't work, but a moment afterwards the door opened by itself, and I felt just as if—no, it's too silly."

"What was it?"

"I felt just as if someone had answered the bell and come into the room."

He hit his forehead with the back of his hand. "Oh, God, are you going to take it into your head that the place is haunted? Don't you like it? Won't it do till we can look for something together? We'll do that as soon as you can walk."

"It's fine," she said. "I like it very much."

"That door's got a way of opening by itself," he said. "I've noticed it before. I think the latch probably needs a drop of oil. I'll see to it."

"Yes, of course that's it."

"And perhaps you were a bit upset by what Mrs. Lambie said."

"Mrs. Lambie?"

"Our neighbour. What she said about not ringing the bell. I expect the journey and then climbing those stairs were a bit too much for you. I've blundered, haven't I, taking this flat? Somehow I can never manage to do the right thing. I'm sorry, I'm sorry!"

He was beginning to work himself up into one of his states of self-accusation, which were really a way of accusing Helen of failing to understand him. She flinched at the thought of the scene that could develop now if she did not manage to stop it in time.

"You're quite right," she said placatingly. "I told you it was silly of me, didn't I? Of course it was just the awful state of nerves I've been in ever since the accident. Perhaps I ought to be on tranquilizers."

"We'd better get you a doctor as soon as possible, anyway. Mrs. Lambie gave me the name of one who lives quite near, who she says is very competent."

"You seem to have been seeing a lot of her."

"I told you, she's been very helpful. She's given me dinner a couple of times and told me a great deal about the neighbourhood. She's got all sorts of stories about it. She seems to have lived here most of her life. In her way, she's very interesting. By the way, she's our landlord. I got the flat through a lawyer who'd advertised in the *Scotsman*, but when I got here it was she who showed me round. Now I'll get those drinks. And don't worry if the door opens. I'll get some oil this afternoon and see to it."

He meant it when he said it, but it was the kind of thing that he forgot to do, and by the afternoon the snow was coming down thickly, covering the pavements and the dark slate roofs of the houses, and Helen did not feel inclined to send him out again into such weather. It turned out that the door would stay shut if it was slammed hard enough. They had an omelet for lunch, and after it Helen went to lie down. The pain in her leg had been dulled by the pills and she soon drifted off to sleep.

Colin did not wake her until six o'clock, when he told her that he had sherry waiting for her and that he had put Mrs. Lambie's chicken casserole to warm up in the oven. They sat by the electric fire in the living-room, with the faded red velvet curtains drawn over the windows, shutting out darkness and snow, and Helen, to her own surprise, found herself in a mood of quiet contentment that she had not known for a long time. Not for many months before they had decided to return to Europe.

Not for at least a year, when that woman Naomi had come into their lives.

But she was thousands of miles away now and Helen had Colin to herself, and at last he seemed satisfied that it should be so. The unfamiliar, gracious room, with the dim light almost concealing the cracks in the plaster and the patches on the wall-paper where someone else's pictures had hung, began to feel strangely homelike.

Mrs. Lambie appeared in the door next morning, carrying a plate of beautifully cut little three-cornered sandwiches. Colin was not there. He had gone out shopping with a list that Helen had made out for him. He was not working at present. He was a schoolmaster, a teacher of history, and the Christmas holidays had begun. So far he had said very little of how it felt to be facing the teaching of Scottish children in one of Edinburgh's more distinguished schools after five years of teaching in East Africa, but it was Helen's impression that he was looking forward to it with some eagerness, though the thought of it intimidated him a little.

The snow had stopped, but there had been a heavy frost in the night and the roofs of the houses opposite were a shining white, in which small rainbows of colour were trapped, under a blue, cloudless sky. Helen had stood at the window to watch Colin set out and had seen him skid and nearly fall on the icy pavement. Apparently it was the morning that the rubbish van came round, for there were two rows of dust-bins along the edges of the pavements, some of them with their contents spilling out into the gutters. They detracted from the dignity of the street and gave it an air of squalor. At one of the bins a lean, black cat was trying to extract what looked like the backbone of a herring, and at last succeeding, sat there, chewing it with great satisfaction. It was as she saw this that Helen heard the front door bell ring.

Using her two sticks, she hobbled along the hall to answer it, and found Mrs. Lambie standing there, holding the plate of sandwiches.

"I do hope I'm not intruding, but I thought these might help you with your lunch," she said, "though I'm not sure if they're substantial enough for a gentleman. There's just pâté inside them, which I made myself, so I can assure you there's nothing unwholesome in them."

Her accent took Helen back to her childhood in Edinburgh. Fully dressed, Mrs. Lambie seemed a different person from the grotesque figure who had peered out from her doorway the morning before and had spoken so mysteriously. She looked about eighty, with a small, pointed, deeply wrinkled face, but a straight back and slim, straight legs with excellent ankles. She was a small woman and very trim, and was dressed in a neat gray tweed suit with a cameo brooch on her lapel and a string of small pearls round her throat. The red hair, which yesterday had fallen in a tangle over her forehead, was brushed smoothly back from it into a small bun. To Helen's surprise, she realised that its colour was its own. The day before she had assumed that it was dyed, but now she could see that there was enough white mixed into it for that not to be possible.

"You're very kind," she said. "Won't you come in? My husband's out at the moment, but he'll soon be back."

The old woman accepted the invitation with an air of eagerness, walking ahead of Helen into the sitting-room.

"He's so charming," she said. "I took a fancy to him at once. And you're both young. I like that. I like having young people living next to me. But of course you won't stay. Nobody stays long in this flat, isn't it strange? I've made it as nice as I can and the rent isn't high, but still they don't stay. Sometimes I wonder if it's something to do with that old murder, that there's still a feeling of evil in the place. Do you think that could be possible? Do you believe in that sort of thing?"

She spoke in as matter-of-fact a tone as if she had just mentioned some minor fault in the plumbing, but her blue eyes, on Helen's face, were watchful. They were very fine eyes. Helen thought that when Mrs. Lambie had been young, she had probably been very striking to look at.

Hoping that she too sounded calm about it, Helen said, "Murder? In this flat?"

"Yes, indeed. Of course it happened long, long ago. These houses are very old, you know. All kinds of things must have happened in them."

Helen had taken the plate of sandwiches and put it down and they sat down on either side of the fire.

"About two hundred years old, aren't they?" she said.

Mrs. Lambie nodded. "And in those days these two flats were all one. I had it divided myself when I bought it after my dear husband died, because of course it was far too big for just me, but it was cheap and really so handsome, I couldn't resist it. And I've always liked this part of Edinburgh. It's got a special sort of character of its own. And I thought I could make a little extra income by letting this half, but people don't stay. Yet I've never felt anything wrong in my own flat. I'm very fond of it."

"What happened?" Helen asked. "Who was murdered?"

"A young woman, the wife of a young advocate. He was very handsome and she was very jealous, because she was older than he was and rather plain, and consumptive too, as so many people were in those days, and they had a maid who was very beautiful, with whom he soon fell in love. And the lady of the house did everything she could to get rid of the maid, but her husband wouldn't have it, so the lady did her best to make the maid leave of her own accord, ringing that bell for her over and over again, and abusing her, and at last the girl told her master that she couldn't stand it any more and was leaving, and he fell into a great rage and threw his wife down the stairs, and she broke her neck and died."

"And what happened to him and the girl?" Helen asked.

"Well, he was executed, naturally. They hanged people in those days. And the girl went nearly mad with grief, and the story is, as it was once told to me long ago by an old neighbour, that if you ring the bell there, she answers it, because she wants revenge on her mistress."

"But it was her mistress who was killed," Helen said. "Wasn't that revenge enough?"

"But it was all her fault, don't you see, because she was so jealous? Jealousy's a terrible thing."

"So that's why you told us not to ring the bell." Helen was rather wishing that she had not heard the story.

The old woman gave a cheerful little laugh. "But of course it wasn't necessary. I can see you aren't at all superstitious. I've never felt at all worried here myself. But then I'm not in the least bit psychic, and I don't know what to think about the people who say they are. Is there any truth in it? I honestly don't know and I should never go so far as to deny it's possible that some people experience things that the rest of us don't. But I thought the story would interest you anyway. Tell me about your accident now. Your husband mentioned it, of course, and told me how helpless you'd be for a time, so that's why I've been trying to help. I believe in helping other people whenever I can. I'll always do anything for anyone."

"It was my own fault really," Helen said. "When we got to London we bought a secondhand car and drove up to stay with some friends of ours who live in a village near Birmingham. I was doing the driving, and I had a feeling there was something wrong with the brakes, not seriously wrong, but I thought we ought to have them seen to. And my husband said he'd attend to that, and I thought he had, and I took the car out one day and its brakes went and I went slap into a lorry that was coming out of a turning when I had the right of way, and I couldn't stop myself. The car was a write-off, of course, and I was lucky to get off with only a broken leg and shock. I was taken to hospital, then I stayed on for a time with our friends, but I didn't feel it was fair to stay with them for ever, so I came after Colin, who'd come on ahead of me to find somewhere for us to live."

Mrs. Lambie looked at her thoughtfully. "And he found something for you at the top of three flights of stairs, and he hadn't had those brakes seen to when he said he was going to. I'm afraid he isn't the most practical of people, is he? But so charming. I understand how easily you can forgive him when that accident certainly wasn't your fault, but his."

"Oh, I don't think so," Helen said. "He'd never told me he'd had the brakes put right, I just took it for granted he had."

"But didn't he know you were going to take the car out? Shouldn't he have warned you?"

Helen gave a worried shake of her head. "I can't really remember. Perhaps he did and I forgot about it. Everything about that time's a bit hazy."

"Yes, of course. Most natural. But such a misfortune, when you were coming to start your new life here. Well, let me know if there's ever anything I can do to help. I can easily go shopping for you. It isn't the sort of thing that gentlemen like to do, though of course they do it much more willingly now than they did when I was young. And I know your husband would do anything for you, even if he's a little thoughtless sometimes. Such very attractive young men sometimes get just a wee bit spoilt and grow up a little irresponsible. But you mustn't hold it against him. I'm sure he can't help it. I hope you enjoy your sandwiches."

With further offers of help, she left.

Soon afterwards Colin returned, having omitted to buy the oil for the latch of the sitting-room door, although Helen had put it on her list, but with everything else that she had written down. When he realised that he had forgotten the oil, he offered to go straight out again to buy it, but he had snow on his shoes and looked so cold that Helen assured him that it was unimportant, and urged him to come to the fire.

"I've had a visit from your friend Mrs. Lambie," she said. "She's overcome by your charm."

"Splendid," he said, sitting down and holding out his hands towards the glowing bars of the fire. "I'm glad I've not lost my touch with aged ladies. I thought it would be a good idea to get on the right side of her, since you'd be stuck up here alone so much and she might easily be useful."

"She told me we've got a resident ghost—did she tell you that?" Helen asked.

"No," he said. "What kind of ghost?"

"Believe it or not, a live-in maid, who comes when you pull that bell." She nodded towards the pretty little bell-pull with its wreath of rosebuds. "Which reminds me, what are we going to do about cleaning this place? I don't know how soon I'll be able to cope with it."

He did not answer at once, but after a moment, looking at her with a troubled frown, he said, "You're worried, aren't you? You're pretending to laugh at it, but yesterday you pulled that bell and the door opened and you were quite frightened, and you're remembering that now."

"No, that was nothing," she said. "I was just startled."

"Why is this woman supposed to haunt the place?" he asked.

Helen told him the story of the old murder, as Mrs. Lambie had told it to her.

The frown deepened on Colin's face. "I wonder why she told you that story, not me," he said. "The other night, when I had dinner with her, she told me a number of fairly gruesome stories about Edinburgh. She seems to like them. She told me the old Burke and Hare yarn, of course, and how the senate room of the University is built over the site where they murdered Darnley, and a particularly nasty story of how some idiot son of a local nobleman roasted a scullion on a spit. And sometimes I got the feeling that her sense of time was all mixed up and that she wasn't sure these things hadn't happened yesterday. But she never told me anything about our domestic ghost."

"She may have been afraid she'd frighten you off the place. As I said, she's really taken to you."

"But she doesn't mind frightening you."

"Or even enjoyed it. Actually I'm more afraid of being haunted by Mrs. Lambie herself than by her ghost. She says people never stay in this flat. It could be, couldn't it, that they have to put up with just a bit too much of Mrs. Lambie?"

"But she *is* awfully helpful," Colin said. "You were asking what we're going to do about cleaning the flat. Well, of course, I can manage that, but I met her on the staircase just now and she told me the address of an agency where we may be able to get a daily. I'll go and see them this afternoon—no, I'll have to leave it till tomorrow. This afternoon I'm going to go and see that doctor she told me about. We want him to come and see you as soon as possible."

"Damn the woman, is she going to run our lives?" Helen exploded, suddenly unaccountably angry. "Can't we do anything without her?"

He gave her a startled look, and they stared at one another blankly. Then Colin's face assumed his deeply hurt look, which changed almost at once into one of rage, and in a high, furious voice, he cried, "Christ, you're jealous of her! She's eighty at least, but you're jealous of her! You can't stand it if I talk to anyone. If this sort of thing goes on, don't you realise what it's going to do to us? I can't stand it—get that into your head—I can't stand it!"

"But of course I'm not jealous of her," Helen said, "and I'm sure she means well. It's just that if I have to have too much to do with her, I may go slightly mad."

"That's the kind of thing you said about Naomi. And that's why we're here—just to get away from Naomi. I told you she meant nothing to me—"

"You meant plenty to her," she interrupted swiftly.

"Did that matter? Could I help it? And didn't I agree to come here just to satisfy you that the thing wasn't important?"

"I thought we came here because we'd agreed there was no future for whites in Africa."

"Oh yes, that's what we told everyone else. But Naomi was the real reason. And now you're jealous of an old woman of eighty, who's only been doing her best to help us."

"Well, d'you realise she tried to put it into my head that my accident was your fault, even though I'd told her it was mine? Is that helping us?"

"So that's it! That's the grievance you've been nursing against me all this time! I knew there was something. But didn't I tell you not to take the car out till I'd had the brakes checked?"

"You know, I thought you'd had them seen to. You didn't try to stop me taking it out."

"I didn't know you were going to."

"I could have been killed."

"And you think I wanted that!"

They were equally angry, but while Colin's voice had stayed loud, Helen's was low and bitter. As she always did, once she had become involved in a quarrel with him, she almost at once started wondering desperately how to put a stop to it. She could have drawn back from it herself in an instant, apologising, even grovelling, but once Colin was sufficiently angry, it took hours,

sometimes even days, to persuade him to forget it. He was looking at her with a strange look in his eyes, which she found
peculiarly disturbing.

"I'm not a murderer," he said, suddenly speaking only just
above a whisper, "but for God's sake, don't provoke me too far."

Then he picked up the overcoat that he had dropped on a
chair, struggled into it and walked out of the room. Helen heard
the outer door slam as he let himself out of the flat.

She knew that he would be gone for most of the rest of the
day, perhaps going to a cinema, or pottering about bookshops,
or merely walking along the slushy streets, encouraging the
black mood that had gripped him, assuring himself over and
over again that he was in the right, which, as it happened, this
time he really was, or so Helen thought, as she turned her anger,
once he was gone, against herself. Of course Naomi had been
the real reason why they had come home. And hadn't she sworn
to herself that whatever happened she would never blame him
for her accident? If she loved him, she had to accept him as he
was, moody, casual, forgetful, but after his fashion loving her.

Or could that be wrong?

Sooner or later, after one of their quarrels, she always arrived
at this point. Did he really love her, or did he merely feel entan-
gled in something from which he could not break free? Was
that the explanation of his moods? Did they mean something far
more important than she had ever let herself believe?

She ate most of Mrs. Lambie's sandwiches for her lunch. She
was halfway through them when she heard the rattle of the letter-box, and leaning on her sticks, made her way along the hall
to the front door to see what had been delivered. One letter lay
on the mat inside the door. She picked it up, looked at the address on it, then grew stiff with shock. It was addressed to Colin,

and the handwriting was Naomi's, and the postmark was London.

For a moment Helen could not believe it, thinking that she must be mistaken about the handwriting. But she knew it well. There had been a time when Naomi, who had been a secretary working for the High Commission, had been her friend rather than Colin's, and Helen had often had notes from her. It was a distinctive writing, not easily mistaken.

Limping slowly back to the sitting-room, she put the letter down on a table, where it would catch Colin's eye when he came back again, then returned to the sandwiches.

Dusk came early, only halfway through the afternoon. The days were just at their shortest. Going to the windows to draw the curtains against the deepening darkness, Helen stood for a moment, gazing down into the street, which just then was empty of traffic. She thought how noble the old houses looked when the light was too dim to show up their state of decay. It was easy to imagine coaches driving along the street, and fine ladies alighting from them and sweeping grandly in at one of the handsome old doorways.

But then, as she drew the curtains, she found herself thinking of a young woman who had once lived here, and perhaps had worn a hoop and powdered her hair, and who might have stood at this window long ago, just as Helen was doing now, watching for her husband to come home, then perhaps seen him hurrying along, but not for her sake. A young woman who had gone to her death down the long stone stairs, because of her jealousy.

Helen looked at the envelope lying on the table and felt an impulse to destroy it and say nothing to Colin about its having arrived, but the impulse was followed by a chilling little tremor of fear. Leaving the envelope lying where it was, she sat down and picked up a newspaper that Colin had brought in with him, and did her best to read.

The doctor called soon after four o'clock. Though Colin had not returned, he had not omitted to call on the doctor recommended by Mrs. Lambie and ask him to visit Helen as soon as possible. He was a short, square man, with a loud, hearty manner, full of reassurance. He wanted the address of the doctor who had treated Helen after her accident, so that he could send for her x-rays and records. Then he stayed chatting for a little, commiserating with her for living at the top of a staircase that would keep her virtually a prisoner until the plaster came off her leg, and for the weather that had welcomed her to Edinburgh. Then he went away, saying that he would call again in a few days.

Colin returned about six o'clock, with a parcel of fish and chips for their supper. He said nothing about how he had spent the day, and looked tired and sullen. Seeing the letter on the table, he ripped it open, read it quickly, then held it out to Helen.

"Here, d'you want to read it?" he asked.

"Not unless there's some reason why I should," she answered, looking away.

He tucked the letter into his pocket and said no more about it.

He was not openly antagonistic to her that evening, but he hardly spoke. They went to bed early. In the morning, soon after he had washed up the breakfast things for her, he left the flat, without telling her where he was going or when he would be back. Helen would have given a great deal at that time to be able to leave the flat too, to be able to go rapidly down the stairs and along the street to investigate the local shops and perhaps take a bus to Princes Street and see how much everything had changed since she had been here last. She felt restless and tense. There had been a partial thaw in the night and most of the white covering of the roofs had slid down on to the pavements, lying there in dirty heaps, but the sky looked low and heavy, as if more snow might be coming soon. Helen sat down in her usual place, near to the electric fire, and wondered how she was going to pass the time.

It was only a few minutes later that she felt the draught on her neck which meant that the door behind her had swung open. It did it so silently that she still found it eerie. Looking towards it and gripping the arms of her chair, she started to heave herself to her feet so that she could go and close it. But as she did so, a slim, ethereal figure in grey moved into her line of vision in the hall. She dropped back into her chair, wanting to scream, and shuddering from head to foot in helpless panic.

The figure moved forward.

"Did I startle you, dear?" she asked. "I'm sorry. The gentleman gave me the keys and said it would be all right if I came straight in, else I might disturb you."

She was a young woman of about twenty-five, tall and vigorous-looking, with short auburn hair and a bright, healthy complexion, and she was wearing a transparent white plastic raincoat, which she started to unbutton as she came into the room. Under the coat she was wearing dark brown slacks and a heavy Aran sweater. She was not in the least ghost-like.

"I said to the gentleman, I said I'm not sure you should give me the keys," she said. "Who kens, I might be anybody, you never ken what I might do with them, but he said it would be better than having me ring the bell and making you come tae the door with your sore leg, and he seemed tae think he could trust me. So I came in, like he said, and if you'll just tell me what you want me tae do, I'll get ahead with it."

"Who are you?" Helen demanded. "What are you talking about?"

"My name's Mrs. MacNab," the girl answered. "but most folks call me Fiona."

"Why have you come?"

"Because I just happened tae meet the gentleman in the agency yesterday afternoon, when I went in tae see if they'd a wee job for me, and he said how you couldn't get around yourself because of your leg being broken, and he wanted someone tae keep the flat clean and I said I could manage, and he gave me the keys and I let myself in, like he said. Were you not expecting me?"

"Yes—yes, of course I was," Helen said. "I'd just forgotten about it. I don't think he told me what time you'd be coming, or if he did, I didn't remember. It's very good of you to come."

"He was so awful anxious about you, I couldn't say no to him," the girl said. "Now, where will I start?"

"Oh, anywhere you like. If you can, just give the place a general clean-up. That would be fine."

"Will do," the girl said cheerfully, and disappeared to the kitchen to look for brooms and dusters.

Helen found herself wanting to laugh helplessly, but she felt that there was a danger of hysteria getting into the laughter and took hold of herself, not to let it escape her. How like Colin it was to have taken the girl on after only a few minutes' talk in an employment agency, almost certainly without asking a single question about her references, and then, on the spot, to have handed over the keys of the flat, and then to have said nothing to Helen about what he had done. That had probably been because when he had returned to the flat the evening before he had still been angry with her, and had half hoped that the girl's sudden appearance would frighten her. He could sometimes be remarkably cruel. But also it demonstrated to her that even when the two of them had quarrelled, he could still be magnanimous enough to go to the trouble of finding this girl to help her.

And of course he had charmed the girl. It had not been concern at Helen's helplessness that had brought her here to work this morning, but Colin's smile, his diffidently courteous manner, his appearance of interest in her. Helen had seen this in operation so often that she could imagine exactly how the scene had gone. She herself was the only person on whom he hardly ever troubled to exercise his charm, and when he did, she found that she had lost the ability to respond to it. She preferred him to be what she considered his natural self, with all his difficult moods, since she was accustomed to them and thought that she understood them reasonably well.

Halfway through the morning Fiona brought her a cup of coffee, then stayed to chatter about herself for a time. She was an unmarried mother with a child of five, she said, whom she had left for the morning in a nursery school. She spoke of the child's father with an amused kind of contempt, but no bitterness, seeming to be glad that he had removed himself from her life. With only a little more warmth she mentioned someone whom she called her boy-friend. Her attitude to men seemed to be placidly uncomplicated. Helen envied her. When the girl had gone, promising to come again in three days' time, Helen thought how comic it had been to confuse someone so robust, even for a moment in the dim light of the hall, where she had looked grey and wraith-like, with the beautiful maid of long ago, who had been the cause of murder.

Colin again returned to the flat at about six o'clock in the evening, bringing with him some packages of Chinese carry-out food, and told Helen that he had spent the day in the National Library, reading up on Scottish social history.

"It's appalling how little I know about it," he said. "If you're educated in England, it's extraordinary how little you learn about the rest of the British Isles. I've a lot to catch up on."

He seemed to be in a better mood this evening than he had been the evening before, glad that Fiona MacNab had arrived to clean the flat, as she had promised, and he presented Helen with two paperback thrillers that he had bought for her during the day.

"You must be getting pretty bored," he said. "Isn't there any-one here whom you used to know in the old days whom you could ask to come and see you?"

"I thought of trying that," she said, "but it's more than ten years since we moved away and I haven't kept in touch with anyone."

"Let's see, all the same."

But something gave Helen the feeling that he was forcing himself to be amiable, to make up for their quarrel the day before, and when they had eaten their king prawn chow mein and drunk some tea, he seemed to have forgotten his suggestion. Helen did not remind him of it. When she thought about the schoolgirls whom she had once known in Edinburgh, they seemed utterly remote. Even if they still lived here, they had very likely got married and changed their names, and if she tried to find them in the telephone directory, there would be no trace of them. In any case, the chances were that they had completely forgotten her. She must face it, her only acquaintance here was Mrs. Lambie. She settled down to read one of the thrillers that Colin had brought her, while he picked up a history that he had bought for himself, but which he left unopened on his knee while he gazed broodingly at the fire.

After a little while, Helen glanced up at him and found that that brooding gaze had been transferred to her face, as if he were asking himself some profound question about her. She smiled and asked him what he had on his mind.

He muttered, "Nothing," and opened his book. But he went on staring at the first page for so long that she knew he was not reading it.

At breakfast next day he told her that he was going back to the library, and as soon as he had done the washing up he left the flat again. He had hardly spoken at breakfast, but once he had gone, the complete silence in the flat seemed suddenly unbearable. Limping from room to room, she tried to fight off a new and terrifying sense of claustrophobia. She had never suffered from it in this way before. It felt as if the walls of the flat were closing in on her and were going to crush her.

The kitchen seemed specially sinister. It had a modern sink and a gas cooker, but the floor was of great, uneven blocks of stone, which must have been there since the house was built, for at no later time would a floor so many storeys up have been paved with such slabs. They were very cold to stand on. Helen found herself thinking of the maid of long ago, so beautiful and so dangerous, who had probably had to live in this kitchen, feel the chill of the floor through her shoes and get down on her knees to scrub it. The thought of her sent Helen back as fast as she could go to the sitting-room, wishing that somehow, if only for a little while, she could get out of the flat and talk to the butcher and the greengrocer and the baker, flesh-and-blood ordinary people who had never driven any man or woman to their deaths.

Going to the window, she wondered if, after all, she made up her mind to it, she could get down the stairs alone and breathe in some of the fresh, cold air of the streets. Getting down should not really be too difficult. She could do it sitting down, manoeuvering herself from step to step without ever putting any weight on her painful leg. It was the thought of trying to get up again without Colin there to support her that she found intimidating. She might actually find it impossible and might have to stay below in the cold for she did not know how long until, if she were lucky, she could persuade some kind passer-by to help her up again.

While she was thinking of this, she saw an old man on the far side of the street slither and fall and lie helplessly where he had fallen on the pavement. It was then that she realised that there had been another heavy frost in the night, and that the half-melted snow of the day before had hardened into a sheet of ice. A passing milkman helped the old man to his feet, brushed him down and made sure that he had not hurt himself before leaving him to go on again down the street, holding tightly to the iron railings of the areas as he went. But the sight had put Helen off any thought of trying to go out herself. She must accept the fact, she was imprisoned here in this silent dwelling.

If only it had not been so silent! If only she could have heard other people moving about in it!

Knowing how foolish she was being, but all at once exasperated beyond bearing, she crossed to the fireplace, grasped the bell-pull beside it and wrenched it and wrenched it over and over again, feeling as if, sooner or later, if only she went on long enough, it would make some sound. Then suddenly it did. A bell pealed clearly in the silence.

She snatched her hand back from the bell as if it had burnt her. Then she realised that of course it was not this bell that had rung, but the front door bell. Leaning on her sticks, she made her way along the hall to the front door and opened it. As she had expected, it was Mrs. Lambie who stood there, dressed in her neat grey tweed suit and holding a saucepan.

"I've just been making a pot of lentil soup," she said, "much too much for just myself, and I thought in this weather you might find it acceptable. There's nothing like a good soup when the weather's so inclement. Do you care for it?"

"How very good of you," Helen said. "Won't you come in?"

"Are you sure it's not inconvenient? I don't want to intrude." Mrs. Lambie was already inside the door by the time she spoke. Helen closed it behind her. "You'll find there's nothing unwholesome in it, none of that tinned stuff, just good ham bones and lentils and plenty of vegetables. I hope you enjoy it. And I hope you and your delightful husband are happy here. I know it isn't very grand, but I did my best to make it comfortable."

"It's fine," Helen said, taking the saucepan and carrying it to the kitchen, then rejoining Mrs. Lambie, who had gone into the sitting-room and sat down by the fire. She was patting her red hair, so bizarre above her aged face.

"Yes, I did my best," she said, "but you aren't happy here, are you? I can always tell. You won't stay."

"Well, of course we never meant to stay for long," Helen said. "As soon as I can get about better we want to find ourselves a small house somewhere and have our own furniture moved in. We had it sent to Edinburgh when we left to come home, and it's in store now."

"Yes, yes, your husband made that quite clear to me when we signed the lease," Mrs. Lambie said. "I knew you'd only be here temporarily. But when I said you aren't happy here, that isn't what I meant. It's nothing to do with the flat, is it? There's trouble between the two of you, anyone can see that. So sad, when you're both so charming. And you're both trying so hard to make a success of things now. I think that's what I noticed first, how hard you were trying. It didn't seem quite natural. Of course I realise you may think I'm very interfering, but I'm a very old woman and I always say what I think now, and I know that sometimes it's a help to have someone to talk to, even someone like me. So tell me, my dear, was the trouble another woman? Was that the real reason why you left Africa, and why you think your husband let you take that unsafe car out on purpose?"

"On purpose?" Helen said sharply. "Whatever made you think that?"

"It's the truth, isn't it?"

"No, of course not. I've never thought of such a thing."

"Dear, dear," Mrs. Lambie said with a sigh. "How very sad. Because it's what your husband thinks himself, you know. He says you blame him for your accident. He told me so himself only yesterday."

"Yesterday?" Helen said.

"Yes, when he dropped in for a drink with me when he got back from the library. I happened to be coming up the stairs myself when he got home and I asked him in for a chat. And we had a wee drink together. I do so enjoy company for a wee drink. It isn't the same when you're by yourself. And he told me how you blamed him for not having had the brakes of the car seen to, just as I was saying to you the other day. And he said how angry you were with him for taking a flat at the top of so many stairs and how you'd stopped trusting him in any way. And I asked him if the real trouble was another woman, because that's what it generally is, and he didn't answer, but I could tell from the way he coloured up that I'd hit on the truth. Oh dear, it's so sad. He's so very unhappy about it. If only I could persuade you not to blame him, because young men like him can't help attracting women, you know. They'll always pursue him. There are people who are like that without meaning any harm, women as well as men. They can't help it. So if you can't make up your mind to put up with it, you'll never be happy yourself. Do take my advice and try to conquer your jealousy. There's been enough unhappiness in this flat because of jealousy. I told you all about that, didn't I—about the young advocate and the beautiful maid? Yes, I remember I did. Well, we don't want any more tragedy here, do we?"

Helen had been only half listening to what the old woman had been saying. She had taken in the fact that Colin had visited Mrs. Lambie the evening before when he returned from the library, had apparently unburdened himself to her, and then had said nothing about this to Helen. And the fantastic thing about this was that what Helen felt about it was a kind of jealousy. That he should have kept the visit to himself made it seem important, overwhelming her for a moment with as deep a fear of losing him as she had ever felt when she had known that he was with Naomi. For if he was afraid to tell her such a thing, it must mean, surely, that she had completely lost his confidence.

Determined above all things that the old woman should not see how she had been shaken, she asked, "Wouldn't you like a drink now, Mrs. Lambie?"

"No, no, thank you, it's much too early in the morning for me," Mrs. Lambie replied. She stood up. "I hope you enjoy the soup. I'm very fond of a good lentil soup myself, and it's as easy to make a big potful as a small one. And think over what I've been saying, because I've had a great deal of experience of life and I know what I'm talking about. Good-bye for now. Don't bother to come to the door. I'll let myself out."

Helen let her do so, then got to her feet and poured out the drink for herself that Mrs. Lambie had refused. Before she drank it, she took two of her pills. Her leg was hurting more than usual. Nerves, she thought. She had actually let that old creature upset her.

Colin came home earlier than he had the day before, bringing with him a cold roast chicken and the makings of a salad. It would have been a chilly meal for such an evening, if it had not been for the lentil soup. As they sat drinking sherry before it by the fire, Helen told Colin how Mrs. Lambie had brought it to her in the morning.

He smiled and said, "She's a kind old thing really, isn't she?"

"I think she's horrible!" Helen said with sudden violence. "She's been doing her best to put evil thoughts into my mind."

"Aren't they there already?" he asked with an edge on his voice.

"Don't, don't!" she exclaimed. "I'm getting the feeling she's putting us against one another. And we'd made up our minds to stop quarrelling, hadn't we? We wanted this to be a really new start."

"Of course, but it isn't her fault if it isn't, it's our own."

She gave a sigh. "I know you're right. It's this being cooped up with the snow and everything that's making me unreasonable. I'm sorry, Colin. But d'you know, it was rather funny this morning. I was in a vile mood and I started pulling that bell, as if it would ring if only I pulled it hard enough—and suddenly *she* came—Mrs. Lambie—just as if I'd summoned her."

"Coincidence."

"Of course."

"Anyway, the bell there wouldn't have been the one that that woman who got murdered used to ring. I'm pretty sure this is a Victorian thing, not Georgian. The works may be original, the wires and so on, but the bell itself isn't really old."

Helen turned to look at the pretty, painted bell-pull, and her face became thoughtful.

"The fact is, you know," she said, "Mrs. Lambie's never told me when that murder happened. She said it happened long ago, but that could mean anything. It doesn't have to mean two hundred years. Suppose it was only fifty, she might actually have been in Edinburgh herself at the time, and remembered quite a lot about it. Perhaps she even knew the people."

"You're letting it obsess you," Colin said. "I wish you wouldn't."

"It obsesses her."

"Because it's nice and dramatic and she's lonely and old and hasn't much else to think about. Now I'll get that soup, and let's forget the ghosts."

"But if it *did* happen only fifty years ago . . ."

But Helen did not finish her sentence. She was not sure what she wanted to say. It was a new thought to her that Mrs. Lambie might have more knowledge of the murder that had happened here in this building than she had implied and that that perhaps was why she had such a pressing need to talk about it. Perhaps, now that she was old and her own death was close to her, she even wanted to confide in someone some secret that she had nursed all these years.

Helen sipped her sherry and tried to adjust her picture of the people who had once lived here in this flat from the hoops and powdered wigs of the eighteenth century to the brief skirts, flesh-coloured stockings and shingled hair of the nineteen-twenties.

Next morning Colin said again that he was going to the library. Helen nearly asked him to stay at home for a change, partly because she was afraid of the mood of yesterday morning returning once she was left alone, but she knew that he would have nothing to do in the flat, and that if he had nothing to do he would soon become restless and irritable. It was fortunate really that he had found something to interest him in the library.

But was it true that he had?

The question sprang so abruptly into her mind that for a moment it made the room spin about her. But once she had asked it of herself she realised that it had been troubling her since the day before. For if Naomi had arrived in London, as it had been plain from the postmark on her letter that she had, might she not have come the small distance further to Edinburgh? Might Colin not be spending his time with her?

The thought filled Helen with sudden terror, more because she felt that she was losing her grip on herself than because she really believed in it. Yet it might be right. Why should it not be right? And if it was, what was to become of her?

In a mood of needing to distract herself at any cost, she fetched the saucepan that had contained the lentil soup from the kitchen, let herself out of the flat and rang Mrs. Lambie's bell.

There was silence for a little while, then the door opened a few inches and Mrs. Lambie peered out cautiously, just as she had when Helen had first arrived. She was dressed as she had been then, in an old quilted dressing-gown, with her red hair tangled about her face. For a moment she gazed at Helen as if she did not know her, but then she gave a vague little smile and said, "Oh, it's you. I couldn't think who it could be. I'm sorry, I'm not dressed."

"I just came to bring you back your saucepan," Helen said.

"Oh dear, you shouldn't have troubled. Any time would have done. But do come in, if you don't mind everything being in a mess. I haven't started to tidy up yet."

It looked to Helen, when she went into the flat, as if Mrs. Lambie had not tidied up for a long time. The room into which she took Helen was very like the sitting-room next door, and it was furnished in much the same way, but there was thick dust everywhere and cobwebs trailed from the ceiling. There were heaps of old newspapers on the floor and stuffing showed through slits in the worn upholstery of the chairs. A small table had been drawn close to the electric fire and had a cup and a coffee-pot on it.

"Really I'm just having my breakfast," Mrs. Lambie said. "I don't get up very early. I've nothing to get up for. But you'll join me in a cup of coffee, won't you?"

Holding her dressing-gown closely about her, as if it might reveal nakedness if she let it go, she went away to the kitchen to fetch another cup.

Sitting down, Helen looked with interest at a row of photographs on the mantelpiece. All but one were of young men, one in the uniform of a subaltern in the First World War, two or three in the plus fours of the nineteen-twenties, a few more who looked as if they belonged to ten years later, and one who was in the timeless wig and gown of an advocate. The one exception to this parade of youth was the photograph in the place of honour in the centre of the mantelpiece. It was of a man of at least seventy, with a plump, mild face, a bald head and vague, troubled eyes, as if, even at his age, he had not got over finding life a bewildering puzzle.

Mrs. Lambie, returning from the kitchen, saw Helen looking at this photograph.

"Ah, you're looking at my picture of my dear husband," she said. "He was a wonderful man, so good and kind and generous. We'd only been married three years when he had a stroke and died, but I'd been his housekeeper for years before that, and understood him perfectly. The rest . . ." She gave a little laugh. "Well, we all have our memories, haven't we? And they keep me company. They were all very dear to me at different times. It may surprise you now, but I was often told when I was young that I was very beautiful. Now, how do you like your coffee? Cream? Sugar?"

Helen said that she would like it black, without sugar.

"Ah, you're worrying about your figure," Mrs. Lambie said with a smile. "I never had to do that."

She handed Helen her cup. Like all Mrs. Lambie's cooking, the coffee was excellent.

She went on, " 'But beauty passes; beauty vanishes; However rare, rare it be . . .' I kept my looks till I was well into my sixties, you know, and even then I had distinction. So that's why I can tell you so much about the dangers of jealousy, my dear. Women were always jealous of me. It used to make me very unhappy, and truly it wasn't my fault. I couldn't help it if men pursued me. It was just something about the way I was made and not my fault at all. Why, one man even died for me."

Suddenly Helen could not drink any more of her coffee. She put the cup down abruptly. Looking at the photograph of the advocate, she asked, "On the gallows?"

The old woman stared at her blankly. "What did you say?"

"Didn't he die on the gallows? Wasn't he convicted of murdering his wife? Didn't he throw her down those stairs out there, and weren't you the maid who caused all the trouble? Fifty or sixty years ago. And didn't you come back here when the flat was for sale because you couldn't keep away from it? It was the scene of your greatest triumph, the most wonderful memory of all."

Mrs. Lambie let her mouth fall open. She also let her dressing-gown fall open, and Helen saw that under it she was wearing a transparent black nightdress, frilly with lace, a private fantasy of youth and beauty.

"Are you mad, woman?" Mrs. Lambie demanded, her voice trembling a little. "What have I ever done to you since you got here but try to help you? Why do you hate me?"

"You've done all you could to turn my husband and me against one another," Helen said. She stood up, grasping her sticks. "You keep giving us advice, but all it comes to is dropping horrible thoughts into our minds." She hesitated. "I'm sorry —I shouldn't have said that. Perhaps you don't mean to do it. I'd better go."

Mrs. Lambie was on her feet, facing her. "Yes, yes, go. I know your type. You're a wicked, jealous woman, that's what you are. You're jealous of me, even at my age. You're jealous of my past and all that I've had. You've never known what it is to be adored, worshipped. You're a plain, ordinary woman who isn't even sure she can keep her husband's love."

"But you were the maid for whom the handsome young advocate was hanged, weren't you?" Helen said. Suddenly she felt absolutely certain of it. "Isn't that true?"

"Go!" the old woman shrieked at her. "Go!"

Helen turned and limped as quickly as she could to the door. When Colin came home that evening, she told him what had happened. By now she felt quite detached from the scene in the flat next door. It was almost as if it had never occurred.

"I'm sorry," she ended. "I don't know what got into me, but at the time it seemed quite obvious to me that she must have been the maid in the story of the murder. I'm not sure what made me so certain of it—something to do with your pointing out that that bell there isn't really old, and then the photograph of the lawyer. But of course I've no evidence. Only the way she took it makes me feel I may have hit on the truth."

Colin had brought home fish and chips again for their supper. He carried the packages out to the kitchen and put them in the oven to keep warm, then returned to the sitting-room with an unusually grim look on his face. He poured out sherry for them both.

"Tomorrow I'm going house-hunting," he said. "I don't know, perhaps this place *is* haunted. Anyway, I've got to get you out of it, because I think you're going mad. If we stay on, I don't know what'll happen."

"I'm not mad," she said. "Don't you see, it's because of her part in the story that she's so obsessed with it and can't let it rest."

"Did you say that to her?"

"More or less."

"For God's sake, don't say it to anyone else," he said. "It's slanderous in the extreme."

"I never see anyone else," she said.

"No," he said thoughtfully. "Perhaps that's the trouble. Anyway, it's obvious I've got to get you out of here. I don't know what'll happen next if you stay. I'll go looking for another flat tomorrow, and try to find one on the ground floor, so that you can get out for a little when you want to."

"Don't bother," she said. "I'm quite all right here."

"You don't seem to understand," he said. "You're making the situation intolerable."

"But suppose I'm right."

He gave his head an impatient shake. "No, something's got to be done. We can't go on like this, or I'll go crazy myself. Perhaps we ought to talk to that doctor. Anyway, I'll see what I can do tomorrow."

He went out to the kitchen to fetch them their fish and chips.

In the morning he repeated that he was going out to hunt for another flat, and when Helen tried to dissuade him, his face took on a set, obstinate look, which meant, she knew, that there was no chance that he would listen to her. And after all, she realised, it might be that he was doing what would be best for them both. Even if she was totally wrong about Mrs. Lambie, there was not much chance that the old woman would forgive her for what she had said, and living next door to her, with no one else at the top of the long stairs, would become more and more impossible. But when Colin left the flat, saying that he was going straight to a house-agent, Helen followed him out on to the landing.

"Please leave things as they are," she pleaded. "I'm not sure that I could face another move."

"You might have thought of that sooner," he said. "But don't worry. I'll pack our things and get you down the stairs."

"But, Colin—"

"No, we've got to go." His voice began to rise.

"But haven't we signed a lease or something?"

"Oh, we'll lose some money, but what's that compared with peace of mind? I'll try to find something that'll suit you better."

Her voice rose to match his. "Ask Naomi to choose it for you then. She may know better than you what a woman wants."

He had been about to start down the stairs, but he checked

himself, turning to stare at her with a startled look of under-standing.

"So you think she's here," he said. "That's been the trouble all along, hasn't it? You think I deliberately got you cooped up here so that there'd be no danger of your finding out that we were meeting."

"Haven't you been meeting?" she asked. "At least since she wrote to you."

"You should have read that letter when I offered to show it to you," he said, "but you were too bloody proud. You tried to pre-tend you didn't care. Well, what it told me was that Naomi's come home to get married and it said good-bye—quite finally. You need never be afraid of her again. And if you don't believe me, the letter's in the wastepaper-basket in our bedroom. Get it and read it for yourself. And get it into your head that if you can't trust me, we can't go on. I may be a hopeless, useless char-acter, but try to realise that I love you, you damned woman, that I always have! There's never been anyone else."

He turned back to the stairs and went running down them.

Helen stumbled towards them.

"Colin—wait!" she called out. "Please wait! Don't go like that!"

But she only heard his running footsteps on the stone stairs, then the slam of the outer door as he reached the bottom.

Then she felt a pair of hands in the middle of her back and a violent thrust. Her scream as she fell echoed in the empty stair-well, where there was no one to hear her.

It was Fiona MacNab, arriving just afterwards to clean the flat, who found the body. She went out, screaming for the police, who arrived in a panda car after only a few minutes. She told them that she had passed Mr. Benson in the street, that he had been almost running, had been muttering to himself and had seemed to be in a state of extreme excitement.

Mrs. Lambie, when they questioned her before the ambulance arrived, said that she had heard the Bensons quarrelling violently on the landing that morning, that they often quarrelled and that it was very tragic, because they were such an attractive young couple. There had been some trouble about another woman, she believed. Colin was picked up later in the National Library, where he had gone after two or three unsuccessful visits to house-agents. Later Mrs. Lambie went into the flat next door and wandered round it, wondering what she ought to do with the belongings that the Bensons had left in their flat. There were only a few clothes and a few books. If no one appeared to claim them, she decided, she would send them to the Salvation Army.

She felt an agreeable sense of peace. During her long life as maid, as housekeeper, and finally as wife, she had committed several murders, the first of them, of course, having been of that irritating, ailing woman who had kept on ringing the bell for attention, and whose good-looking young husband had been Mrs. Lambie's first love. A pity that they had hanged him, he had really been very attractive. But how could she have helped it? And no one had ever come near to guessing her secret but that wretched girl with her broken leg, who had had too much time on her hands and become fanciful, and so had come too close to the truth for comfort. A pity about her husband too, a nice-mannered young man who understood that even a very old woman enjoys a friendly chat once in a while. But at least they wouldn't hang him. It would only be life-imprisonment.

Letting herself out of her flat, she returned to her own. As she did so, it seemed to her that very faintly she heard a bell ringing. She had often heard it throughout her life, and she knew quite well that it was simply in her own head. But the odd thing was that it still frightened her. One day soon, she felt, it might turn into an imperative summons that she would have to answer, and what would happen then?

AFTER DEATH THE DELUGE

It was six o'clock when Margaret Haddow started to cook the supper. She put potatoes into a basin, ran water over them and started to peel them.

Aged twenty-four, small, inconspicuously pleasant to look at, she had a vitality that made her attractive, and slightly less simplicity than, at a first meeting, might have been supposed. She was wearing grey slacks and a scarlet sweater and had a cigarette at the corner of her mouth.

Peeling the potatoes, she hummed quietly. The tune she hummed was unrecognisable and it is unlikely that she even knew that she was humming. Probably nothing was in her mind at that moment but the thought of the shepherd's pie that she was just starting to make. Perhaps she was thinking that the kitchen felt cold after the well-warmed sitting-room.

But that particular moment, when her potato-peeler was ripping down the side of the second potato and her humming was sounding tunelessly in the small kitchen, was the last moment that evening when thoughts that grew out of her normal life had any room in Margaret's mind.

It was at that moment, just outside the kitchen window, beginning with a few heavy splashes, then turning all at once into a torrent, that something that sounded like the lash of a rainstorm was suddenly released against the glass. But the torrent was all against one window and on to one window-sill. Big drops, bright where they caught the light from the kitchen, spangled the dark square of the window-pane.

Startled, Margaret paused and looked round. As she did so, something ice-cold fell on the nape of her neck. It slid down between her shoulder blades, inside her red sweater. With a gasp and a shudder she jumped aside. As another drop fell she looked up. Through a crack in the ceiling that she had never noticed was there, water was oozing, gathering into another large, dirt-discoloured drop, quivering, preparing to fall.

Seeing where it splashed on the floor, Margaret took a bucket from one of the cupboards and put it on the spot. Another drop and another, each gathering a little more quickly than the last, fell into the bucket. Standing back, watching them fall, Margaret raised a hand to thrust it in bewilderment through her hair. As the hand came level with her face, she felt a freezing drop fall on the back of it.

The second crack oozed water faster than the first. But by the time that she had found a basin to place under it, the first was running freely. Outside the window it was still pouring down. Every instant the force of the stream inside increased. The bucket would not take long to fill.

Suddenly she spun on her heel, pulled open the kitchen door and went running out into the hall.

As she groped for the light-switch, she realised that the whole house was full of the sound of water.

She turned on the light. In this house the flats were not self-contained. All the tenants used the passage in which she was standing. This was the ground floor. The front door was straight before her. From one corner of the ceiling water was spouting, making an increasing puddle on the green linoleum.

Running upstairs, Margaret started calling, "Is anyone there?"

She thumped on each of the doors of the first floor flat.

There was no answer.

She tried the handle of the sitting-room. It was unlocked, as

Paul Wragge's rooms usually were, but the room inside was in darkness. Water was spouting somewhere in the room and from the kitchen beyond she could hear a swirling and splashing.

It was the same on the top floor, except that all the doors were locked and that it sounded as if it were raining everywhere. Turning, she ran downstairs again.

She was almost down to the ground floor when she heard a voice calling, "Mrs. Haddow! Mrs. Haddow!"

A long, pale face with pince-nez and carefully brushed, scanty grey hair was peering up at her over the banisters.

"Mrs. Haddow, whatever shall we do?" It was the tenant from the basement. He was a borough councillor, Chairman of the Baths and Cemeteries Committee, and his name was Ferdinand Shew. "It's come through in my basement in three different places and soon everything's going to be soaked. Soaked! Whatever shall we do?"

"I think the tank in the roof must have burst," she said.

"Oh dear," he said, "oh dear!" His eyes, of a yellowish brown, which might have been cat-like had they not been so vague, were full of apprehension. "Is Mr. Wragge in?"

"No, nor's Mr. Boyle, and he's left his flat all locked up, so we can't go up to the loft to see if there's anything we could turn off."

"How like him. How like him always to be inconsiderate!"

"D'you know where the main tap is, Mr. Shew?"

"No—no, I don't. But come downstairs, Mrs. Haddow, come down to my basement and see how terrible it is. If it goes on, everything's going to be ruined."

She went downstairs with him to the fussily, lacily over-furnished flat where the councillor lived with his housekeeper, Miss Pattison.

Standing in his small hall, a tall, drooping figure in bedroom slippers, he flapped his hands at the runnels of water down his walls, at the pools at his feet. He had placed buckets and basins to catch as much as he could, but the pools were extending over the floor.

"Look, it'll get into the sitting-room soon," he said, "and then it'll ruin things, *ruin* them. I wonder what we can do. I wonder, if you took a mop and I took another, whether perhaps we could stem it. And my poor Miss Pattison's in bed with bronchitis, you know. I've been spending the afternoon so peacefully, reading to her."

Margaret replied, "I've my own puddles to think about."

"But *look* how it's pouring down! And I can't disturb poor Miss Pattison. Just look at it!"

"Isn't there a main tap somewhere down here?" she asked. "There usually is in the basement."

"There *is* a tap of some sort in the coal-cellar," he said. "D'you think that'd be it? I've never turned it on or off, that I can remember, but perhaps I might try. We couldn't make things any worse, could we?"

"Not much," Margaret agreed.

"Very well, I'll try." He disappeared through one of the doors. In a moment he was back.

"There," he said, looking round hopefully at the water that poured with ever increasing force. "Is that any better?"

"It wouldn't get better for some time," Margaret said.

"How awful it is," he said, "how truly awful."

"The next thing," Margaret said, "is to try to get hold of a plumber. D'you know one? I'll go for him—though with the thousands of burst pipes there probably are everywhere, I don't suppose we'll be able to get one."

"Why doesn't Mr. Boyle come home, or Mr. Wragge, or your husband?" moaned Mr. Shew. "Look, Mrs. Haddow, here's a cloth. D'you think you could start mopping up? Look, if you could mop up over there, so that it doesn't spread into the sitting-room . . ."

She said briskly, "Michael won't be home for another couple of hours. And I'm going for a plumber."

"Oh no, *I'll* go for a plumber." He thrust the cloth into her hand. "I couldn't dream of letting you go out at this time of night. I'll go at once. And if only you'd mop up a little . . . You know, it really is like Mr. Boyle to leave things locked up. He's always inconsiderate. And I'm always doing little things to oblige him, but he's most rude and unappreciative—most."

"His place must be in a far worse state than ours." She had stooped and was mopping at the edge of a pool, but it was growing far faster than she could diminish it.

"Perhaps we might be able to get in upstairs somehow," he said, standing watching her. "Suppose I go up and try." Suddenly he gave a giggle. "You know, this is really very amusing. I dare say if we could see ourselves . . . Now, I think I'll just go up and see if I can get in upstairs somehow. I think that's the best thing to do."

She watched him go, then with an irritated gesture, flung down the mop and followed him.

He was saying, "'If seven maids with seven mops . . .' D'you know, Mrs. Haddow, I think it's coming through in your sitting-room too?"

He was right.

"And it's just occurred to me," he went on, "that we ought to turn off the lights, or they'll be going anyhow. Just a minute, I've got a torch downstairs. I'll fetch it. There!" Suddenly the hall was in darkness. "I knew that would happen. Just a moment. I'll get my torch."

He disappeared down the stairs again.

When he returned at last with the torch, Margaret said, "I wish you'd go for that plumber."

"I'm going, I'm going immediately." He started up the stairs.

Muttering, "It's no good whatever," she followed him.

Though Margaret had left all the lights on the staircase burning, it was dark now all the way up. The sound of water pouring through the house was like rain in a forest. The torch cut into the darkness with a long cone of light. They went on up the stairs.

They were almost at the top landing when Mr. Shew exclaimed, "That was my bell ringing. Didn't you hear it?"

"I didn't hear anything," she said.

"I'm sure it was," he said. "Someone at the door. I'd better go down, or Miss Pattison will be getting out of bed to answer it. I can't allow that. It might set her back seriously. You can't think how inconvenient for me it is when she's ill in bed."

Taking the torch with him, he plunged down into the darkness.

Margaret sighed. She stayed where she was, about three steps from the top of the staircase. Her feet were cold inside her soaked slippers. Her hands, encountering dampness whatever they touched, were numb.

There was something uncanny about standing there in that drenched darkness. She started shivering, and it was not all because of the cold. The darkness was so deep, the spouting of all that water around her so unnatural. After about five minutes it was suddenly too much for her. She turned and ran downstairs.

Between the two upper floors there was a half-landing. It was as she reached this that Margaret fell. She did not hurt herself much. Had her weight been flung to the left, the fall might have been a serious one, but it was flung to the right, and instead of toppling down the rest of the flight, she merely bruised her shoulder against the door of a cupboard that opened on to the small landing. Sliding to the floor in front of it, she felt a gush of water full in her face.

The ice-cold water made her disregard the question of how much she was hurt. Scrambling to her feet, she dashed the water from her eyes and hurried on downwards. Ferdinand Shew was back in the hall, putting a package on the shelf by the front door.

"I don't want to complain," he said in a voice shrill with exasperation. "I don't like to disoblige anybody. But that man Boyle has no sense of proportion in the way he imposes on one. He has no thought for others at all. I've just taken in a bottle of whisky for him. Whisky! And he'd had the impertinence to tell them at the shop to take it round to my door because he knew he wouldn't be there to take it in himself. I take his laundry in for him every Friday and put it on the shelf there. Every afternoon of my life I take in his loaf of bread. Why, I should like to know, *why* should I have to come upstairs every afternoon with his loaf of bread? And I pay for all those things too. I've just paid nearly five pounds for this whisky. I don't mean he doesn't pay me back—he does, of course—but it's so selfish of him, so utterly selfish, to assume he can make use of me like that. And then he leaves his door locked and doesn't come home just when he might be useful."

"Mr. Shew, are you going for that plumber?" Margaret asked, rubbing the shoulder that had hit the door.

"I'm going," he said, "immediately, immediately."

"If you don't, I will."

"I'm going, I'm going."

But before it was possible for him to go in search of a plumber, he had to put on a mackintosh and cap and find his umbrella, though the evening outside the house was fine. Margaret went halfway down the stairs into his basement to make sure that he actually set off. The floor of his little hall was a-swim now. His lights, however, were still burning.

Looking up at her, he tittered.

"You look just like the boy who stood on the burning deck," he said. "I wonder, while I'm gone, couldn't you just try mopping up a little? Just a little. Just to stop it spreading into the sitting-room."

Wearily she came downstairs and picked up the mop.

It was as she came into the light that Ferdinand Shew, giving a shrill cry, snatched up one of her hands and exclaimed, "Why, look, Mrs. Haddow, you've hurt yourself!"

"I fell," she said, "but I didn't hurt myself much."

"But you're bleeding."

Margaret pulled her hand away from him and looked at it.

"And on your trousers," he said, pointing.

"But I didn't feel anything," Margaret said.

Yet there was blood on her hands and a long red stain down the side of her slacks.

"I'm *not* hurt," she said. "There's nothing, not a scratch. I bruised my shoulder, but . . ."

She stopped. She lifted her eyes. Slowly they sought those of the councillor.

"Do you think . . . ?" she began.

He was still looking at her hand, at the narrow line of red that was drying round the edge of her fingernail.

"Do you think perhaps," she said, "that we ought to go and see . . . ?"

But she stopped again. There was a curious constriction about her mouth.

"I fell," she managed to say in a whisper, *"on that half-landing."*

"I'll go for the plumber *and* the police," Councillor Shew said when they had seen what the cupboard on the half-landing contained.

At last he seemed in a hurry.

Reminding Margaret that she was not alone in the house—there was Miss Pattison in the basement—he gave her the torch and darted off down the slushy pavement. Margaret went to her sitting-room. Water was pouring into it, the carpet soaking up the pools. The light was still on there, but her gaze saw nothing of the spoiled and streaming walls. As she perched uneasily on the arm of an easy chair, the sensation that gripped her was unlike anything that she had ever experienced. Mr. Shew had told her that for safety she ought to turn off the lights, but nothing, no command, no caution, could have made her reach for the switch.

But she had been sitting there only a few minutes when the light above her head went out. Water came trickling down the cord itself.

Suddenly there was a tearing sound and a crash. Margaret leapt about a yard from where she was sitting. A lump of the ceiling had fallen just beside her chair. As she fled to the doorway, another heavy chunk of plaster came down. Margaret leant against the doorpost. She stuffed her fingers into her mouth, bit into them, almost choked herself with them, while her whole body shuddered.

Gradually the danger of the scream that had almost burst from her receded. All at once she was steady, decided, certain of what she wanted to do.

She went into the kitchen. Rummaging through a drawer, using the torch, she picked out a knife with a long, thin, flexible blade. She went upstairs. Before she came to the half-landing, she was trembling again, but she managed to pass the closed cupboard door and went on to the door of Mr. Boyle's sitting-room, slid the point of the knife in beside the spring lock and did her best to break into his flat.

Because the door was only an old attic door, fitting very loosely, she succeeded.

Mr. Boyle's sitting-room was not as wet as might have been expected. The floor was swimming, but it was through the kitchen ceiling that most of the water was pouring down. Following the beam of the torch, she picked her way amongst the chairs, ashtrays and newspapers into the kitchen. Here she found an untidy litter of about three days' dirty dishes. There was food on the table, a half-empty bottle of milk, a butter-dish, some rashers of bacon, a loaf of sliced bread in a paper wrapper, a jar of marmalade. Everything was drenched in water. The most concentrated stream came from a crack at one corner of the trap-door that led up into the loft.

When she saw that, Margaret gave up. She did not know what deluge might fall upon her if she moved the trap-door. But the expedition had at least distracted her. For a few minutes she had almost forgotten that she shared a solitude with that battered thing in the landing cupboard.

When Mr. Shew returned, coming up from the basement and tapping on the door of her bedroom, where she had taken refuge because as yet no water was leaking into it, he told her that the police would be there immediately, the plumber shortly.

"Mr. Shew," Margaret said, standing steaming in front of the gas fire, "have you ever seen that—that man upstairs before?"

"Never in my life."

"I have."

His eyebrows popped up above the rims of his pince-nez.

She nodded grimly. "Yes, going upstairs with Mrs. Wragge."

"What, before . . . ?"

"Yes, before she left Mr. Wragge."

"Of course, of course." There was an excited gleam in the yellowish eyes. "Well, the police will see to that, no doubt."

"Mr. Shew . . ." She was speaking slowly, thinking between the words. "When I went upstairs the first time . . . the lights were still on. . . . I'm sure. . . . I'm absolutely certain . . . there wasn't any blood on the landing then."

He seated himself on a chair. His mackintosh draped itself in stiff folds around him. "You say you're absolutely sure?"

"Absolutely sure," she said. "The water was spouting hard just above it, and I looked down at the mess it was making on the floor, and I *know* there wasn't any blood there."

"Indeed! That's very interesting." He gave his little giggle. "Playing detectives! Oh dear, if you and I could see ourselves."

"But that means," she went on, "that he could only just have been put there. I mean, if he'd been there any time, the blood would have dried, it wouldn't have trickled out under the door. So someone must have been in the house only just before the water started running. It was just six o'clock when I went into the kitchen to cook the supper and had to stop because of the water coming in."

"I know what you're going to say!" he cried. "I know, I know!" He jerked himself forward to the edge of the chair. "You're going to say that it's always at six in the evening that Mr. Wragge goes to work."

She was nodding when they heard feet tramping on the pavement outside, and a rapping on the front door that echoed through the house.

From the time when Superintendent Cust appeared, accompanied by a sergeant, nothing in the house seemed quite so sinister. There was still the darkness, the drumming water, the tomb-like smell of wet plaster, the puddles on the floor. Upstairs in a cupboard there was still the body of a man with his head battered in. But Superintendent Cust had a square face with brown, rubbery skin. He had a square, heavy body and square-tipped, heavy hands. And he had a way of pulling his features together in a bunch with one hand and speaking through the fingers in a voice so smothered by them that it sounded as if he were suffering from a dreadful cold. His presence brought reassurance.

"Good heavens," he said, "why didn't you tell us we needed umbrellas?"

"It's upstairs, Superintendent," Mr. Shew said, "in an upstairs cupboard."

"Of course it's upstairs. What is it, a burst tank?"

"I mean, the corpse is upstairs—the dead man."

"Oh yes, that. Why don't you turn the main tap off?"

"I've done so. This water is what had already collected in the walls and ceilings. There was no one at home in either of the top floor flats when the pipe, or the tank, or whatever it is burst, so the upper floors had time to become completely flooded before Mrs. Haddow and I were aware of anything amiss."

"Never seen anything like it," Mr. Cust said. He pulled nose, cheeks and chin together into a handful and looked round at the sergeant. "Maybe you could do something about it, Bill," he suggested.

Margaret remarked, "When the plumber comes, I suppose he'll think it's his job to investigate the murder."

Mr. Cust's eyes came round to her. "You the lady who found the body?"

"We both found the body," Mr. Shew said quickly. "It was Mrs. Haddow who slipped in the blood, thus drawing our attention to the fact that there was a body there."

A crash reverberated in the darkness.

"Some more of my ceiling coming down," Margaret said.

"All right," Mr. Cust said. "Well, let's go along up and look at him."

On the way up the stairs he leant towards Margaret and whispered, "Who is the old boy?"

"He's Councillor Shew," she answered, "Chairman of the Baths and Cemeteries Committee."

He gave a muffled whistle.

He gave another whistle when he saw the body.

"That's dead, that is," he said, and after a minute or two, during which his massive hindquarters had concealed most of the cupboard, he added, "Not very long either. Not more than half an hour or so, I should guess."

Mrs. Shew began, "Mrs. Haddow and I have deduced . . ."

But the superintendent went straight on, "Who lives in this flat up here?"

"A man called Boyle," Mr. Shew said. "I believe he deals in electrical apparatus of some sort."

"And down there?"

"A man called Wragge. He's a sub-editor on the *Gazette*."

"Oh, works at night, I suppose."

"Yes, he goes out every evening about six o'clock."

"Out now?"

"Yes."

Mr. Cust went up the stairs to Boyle's flat. He tried all the doors. Finding them locked, he came down to the first floor, tried the handle of the door nearest to him, found that it would open and went in. Margaret and Mr. Shew could hear him moving about inside and caught an occasional glimpse of his light as he flashed it from side to side.

After a moment he called to them, "You said he was out."

"Yes," Margaret said.

"Well, come and have a look here." Mr. Cust's voice came from the bedroom.

As they approached he flashed his torch at the bed. It picked out the haggard face and limp black hair of the man who was lying across it, the counterpane crumpled under him. His arms were flung out on either side, one knee was drawn up, the foot, in a sock through which most of a toe protruded, resting on the edge of the bed. His mouth hung open. Through it he was drawing slow, snorting breaths, while his chest rose and fell laboriously.

"That him?" Mr. Cust asked.

Margaret nodded.

"He often like this?"

"Since his wife left him about three months ago, pretty often."

"And before that too," Mr. Shew said.

Mr. Cust gave some directions to the sergeant. A quantity of cold water that was pouring uselessly through the house was deflected for the purpose of sobering up the journalist. It took time. Even when he had been roused, Paul Wragge's brain seemed to be in a cloud. Recently, whenever Margaret had met him, he had seemed to be in a cloud.

Mr. Cust stood and watched him. When Paul Wragge was sitting up, his head drooping on to his chest, his back a sagging curve, Mr. Cust said, "Been in all day, Mr. Wragge?"

The third time he asked the question he received an answer of sorts.

"Been in? Been—in? I don't know what you're . . . Look here, what the hell's happening?" Paul Wragge's eyes shifted, wincing, from one face to another. "Where's all this water coming from? Why don't you turn it off?"

"This gentleman says he *has* turned it off," Mr. Cust said. "Now, Mr. Wragge, how long have you been in?"

"You're the police," Paul Wragge said.

"That's right."

"I've been in all day."

"Had any visitors?"

"What's the matter with you? What the hell's happening? Why are you asking questions? Isn't a man allowed to get drunk in his own home any more?" Wragge's hands were kneading at his temples.

"If you don't mind," Mr. Cust said, "there's something I'd like to show you."

He put a hand under Paul Wragge's elbow.

He allowed himself to be helped to his feet. He allowed himself, though he walked staggeringly, to be led out on to the landing and up the stairs. He looked where the superintendent's torch pointed.

Margaret had been trying to keep her nerves in order to deal with this moment. But in her imaginings nothing had been so shocking as what actually happened.

Paul Wragge laughed.

"Whoever would think," he said in a drawling voice, "that a thing like that could happen to one twice in a life-time?"

Mr. Cust waited. Paul Wragge merely stood there, staring down.

Mr. Cust said, "Have you ever seen this man before, Mr. Wragge?"

There was a slight pause, then the journalist replied, "I'll tell you something. I'll tell you something that happened to me years ago. I was a reporter. My first job. I was nineteen. I'd been sent along to the local morgue to get some details about a suicide. The sergeant in charge was awfully bright and breezy, chatted along, told me—"

"Mr. Wragge, have you ever seen this man before?"

"—told me all the gory details I wanted. Then suddenly he whipped the cover off one of the corpses. A girl, quite young. She'd got nice, fair hair. And her throat had been cut from ear to ear. He did it just to see me be sick or faint. Nice chap! I didn't do either."

"Have you seen this man before?" Mr. Cust repeated.

Though water was splashing all over him, Paul Wragge showed no desire to move.

"No," he said.

"Would you swear to that?"

"My bell!" Mr. Shew cried suddenly. "My door bell—didn't you hear it? The plumber!" He pelted down into the darkness.

"My God, what a lot of water!" Paul Wragge muttered. "Yes, I'd swear to it."

Mr. Cust said, "I hear your wife left you three months ago."

"Yes," Paul Wragge answered.

Thickly through his fingers came Mr. Cust's next question, "What was the name of the man for whom she left you?"

Paul Wragge's answer was something very short, very obscene. Margaret turned quickly and went downstairs. She stood in her own hall, fighting off a horrible nausea.

After standing there for a minute or two, she went to the door of the basement and called down, "Mr. Shew, I'm going to make some tea."

"Oh, that's really kind of you, Mrs. Haddow, very kind." He came pounding to the foot of the staircase. "If you really wouldn't mind. It *is* such a good idea in the circumstances."

Out of the shadows the plumber appeared and stood at Mr. Shew's elbow. He was a small man with a grudging voice and a felt hat tipped so steeply over his face that little of it showed but a drooping moustache.

"You got the main tap turned full on," he said.

"On?" Mr. Shew said. "I turned it off."

"On," the plumber said.

"Off!" Mr. Shew cried.

"You may a meant to turn it off," the plumber said, "but you turned it *on*. *I* turned it off. Now I'll go up and take a look in the loft."

"The top flat's locked," Mr. Shew said. "You can't get in."

"It's all right," Margaret said. "I know how to get in. Come on, I'll show you."

She had to repeat the performance of breaking into Mr.

Boyle's flat under the eye of Mr. Cust, who went in with her and the plumber and stood watching while the legs of the plumber disappeared into the roof. Then he started roaming round the flat. Margaret went downstairs again. She fetched the electric kettle from the kitchen and plugged it into the switch in the bedroom. She fetched the rest of the tea-things on a tray and set the tray down on the floor, squatting on the floor herself, as close to the gas fire as she could without being singed. The kettle came to the boil, and she made the tea, pouring out a cup for herself, sitting there with both hands nursing the hot cup. She kept chewing at her lip, pursuing a thought that dodged round the edges of her mind, but would not let her grasp it.

Presently there was a discreet knock at the door. The councillor put his head round it.

"Ah," he said, "tea!" He came in. "I really think the water isn't flowing quite so heavily, Mrs. Haddow."

She agreed, pouring out tea for him.

"The plumber says it's all turned off now, but the walls and ceilings will take at least an hour to empty. Mrs. Haddow, you'll never tell anyone, will you—*anyone*—about my turning the tap the wrong way?"

She smiled absently, pouring out more tea for herself.

"Though of course it wouldn't have made much difference, would it?" he said. "Most of the damage must have been done already, don't you think? Listen—I really think it's getting less every moment. It seems the main pipe burst. The plumber's seeing to it."

Margaret spoke abruptly. "Are they going to arrest Mr. Wragge?"

"Well, it does look rather like it, doesn't it? Of course, I don't know. But I should think they'd take him along to the police station for questioning." He eyed her thoughtfully. "Do you—er—

happen to know anything about Mr. Wragge's unfortunate private affairs?"

"Only what he poured out on Michael and me one evening when he was a bit, but not frightfully, drunk."

"Did he say anything about the—er—the other man?"

"There wasn't one."

"Dear me, dear me." Mr. Shew stirred his tea and sipped a little, those vague cat's eyes of his behind the pince-nez dwelling on her face.

"You see," Margaret said in an uncertain voice, as if it were rather hard for her to understand what she was saying herself, "it seemed to be just that that was so awful for him. I mean, that she'd just gone away because she couldn't stand living with him. She just left him and went back to her old job."

"And I don't wonder!"

"No, I suppose not," she said, and sighed.

"Listen," he said, "it *is* getting less, isn't it?"

"Yes, I think so."

They sat there, gradually feeling warmer and drier. Bit by bit the swish of water lessened to the pattering of individual drops. Policemen went on walking about upstairs. Their voices sounded on the staircase. Mr. Shew started telling anecdotes.

Presently Superintendent Cust came down and asked Margaret if she had heard anyone leave the house before the water started. She told him that she had had the radio on. Mr. Cust asked Mr. Shew what he had been doing between half past five and six. The councillor said that he had been reading *The Wind in the Willows* to his housekeeper, Miss Pattison, who was ill in bed with bronchitis.

Mr. Cust left them and Mr. Shew went on with his anecdotes.

The deluge was almost at an end. It was only a drip-drip from corners and ceiling cracks, when Margaret heard the sound of a key turning in the front door.

She leapt towards it, calling out, "Michael!"

But the sergeant was there before her and when the door opened it was not Michael Haddow who stood there, but Philip Boyle.

He was a short man, slight and wiry, with stiff fair hair that stood up in a brush. His face was a rather red one, with bushy fair eyebrows, hard blue eyes and a small moustache. His manner, which had the assertiveness and suspiciousness of a man who never forgot his rights, was markedly uncordial. He was wearing a loose tweed overcoat of loud pattern and carried a dispatch-case.

Stepping inside, he started rubbing his shoes on the mat.

The sergeant said, "Shouldn't bother with that if I was you. Place is in a worse mess than you can make it in. Who is he, miss?" He looked over his shoulder at Margaret.

"It's Mr. Boyle, the top floor tenant," she replied.

Philip Boyle stared at the sergeant. "What's happened?" he demanded.

"Burst pipe," the sergeant said. "Come along in, Mr. Boyle. The superintendent will be glad to see you."

Philip Boyle looked past the man at Margaret.

"What's happened?" he repeated sharply.

She shrugged her shoulders slightly and said nothing.

With a look of irritation on his face, Philip Boyle strode forward, and the sergeant, coming immediately after him, called up to Mr. Cust that the man from the top floor had just come in. Leaving Mr. Shew to a fourth cup of tea, Margaret followed them upstairs.

Someone had placed candles on the staircase and landings. In their soft light the devastation of the house had lost its menace, but the amount of destruction showed clearly.

Mr. Cust came to meet Philip Boyle. He greeted him, "A grim homecoming for you this evening, Mr. Boyle."

"What *is* all this about?" Boyle's voice was naturally harsh. "What's happened? Does one have to have police in to deal with a burst pipe?"

The plumber sidled past them. "*I'm* here to deal with the burst pipe," he said. "Joseph Loveday, Plumber and Practical Builder. There's a hole in the main pipe up there big enough to stick your three fingers through."

He went on downstairs.

Mr. Cust stood aside so that Philip Boyle could see into the cupboard.

"This is why we're here, Mr. Boyle."

In Margaret's head at that moment there woke echoes of the laughter with which Paul Wragge had greeted the dead man. It was her impulse to plunge downstairs immediately. But suddenly she realised that Paul Wragge himself was standing beside her. He was a tall man whose wide shoulders should have been squarer than they were, whose fine-drawn features should never have been ravaged by the fiend-ridden imagination that possessed him.

As if she had some responsibility concerning him, Margaret stayed where she was.

But there was no laughter in Philip Boyle's reaction to what he saw. He simply clutched the banisters and looked as if he wanted to be sick.

"Have you ever seen this man before?" the superintendent asked.

Taking a handkerchief from his pocket, Boyle wiped it over his mouth. He glanced down at the dead man once more and then away again.

"Yes," he said.

"Do you know him?"

"I—I met him for a few moments once. I don't know his name."

"Where did you see him?"

Philip Boyle turned slightly so that his back was towards the landing below where Paul Wragge and Margaret were standing.

"In Mr. Wragge's flat."

Margaret glanced quickly at Paul Wragge. He made no movement.

Mr. Cust said, "Oh, in Mr. Wragge's flat? How long ago?"

"I forget."

"Please try to remember."

"I can't. I just remember his face. Perhaps it was six months ago."

"And now, Mr. Boyle," Mr. Cust said, bunching up his face in his fingers, "would you mind telling me where you were this afternoon between half past five and six?"

"Was—was that when it happened?"

"Where were you?"

"In my office, of course."

"Was anyone with you?"

"My secretary, and George Lumley, my partner."

"They'll corroborate that?"

"Of course."

"Would you please tell me where I can get in touch with them?"

Philip Boyle was just starting to give the name of his secretary when, from downstairs, the voice of the borough councillor rose up to them out of the darkness.

"Mr. Boyle," Mr. Shew called, "I paid four pounds and seventy-nine pence for that whisky you had delivered this evening. You won't forget it, will you? I paid four pounds and seventy-nine pence. It's here on the shelf by the front door."

Philip Boyle was continuing, "Her name's Adela Burton and—"

But that was the moment when the thought that had been dodging on the outskirts of Margaret's mind suddenly surrendered itself to the grip of her understanding.

"Don't believe him!" she cried. "It isn't true! He was here this afternoon. He was in his flat."

She came running up the stairs.

He went on, "Miss Adela Burton, Seven Milbury Road—"

"It isn't true!" Margaret cried again. "If she corroborates it, she's in it too. He was here this afternoon."

The superintendent took his hand away from his face, allowing his nose, cheeks and chin to settle back into their proper places.

"What's this, Mrs. Haddow?" he asked. "What are you trying to tell me?"

"The bread," she said, "the loaf of bread in his flat. It's there in a paper wrapper that hasn't been opened, on his kitchen table. But the baker's van always calls in the afternoon and Mr. Shew takes the bread in for him and puts it on the shelf by the front door. But it isn't there now, it's in his flat on the kitchen table. He came in and picked it up and took it upstairs with him. It couldn't have been done by the woman who cleans up for him. She hasn't been here today. The place is full of dirty dishes. It *must* have been him!"

Philip Boyle's face had turned a congested crimson. "That's yesterday's bread," he said.

"Ask Mr. Shew," Margaret retorted. "Didn't he take a loaf in for you this afternoon and put it on the shelf, and is it there now?"

Philip Boyle swung his arm, aiming his fist at her face. But it never came near her. Mr. Cust caught it and forced it down to his side.

Releasing it, the superintendent said, "Your coat's damp too, Mr. Boyle, and it hasn't rained *outside* this evening."

Two days later Superintendent Cust explained to the Haddows and to Ferdinand Shew the parts of the situation that they did not understand.

"Boyle met him in Wragge's flat all right," he told them, "but met him again later and got to know him pretty well. He's a man called Winters. He lent Boyle money for his business. I don't believe Boyle meant to kill him when he brought him to his flat that afternoon, but Winters was demanding his money back and Boyle lost his head and lashed out. He lashed out with a stool, a heavy wooden thing he's got up there in his sitting-room. And then the water started coming through the ceiling, and Boyle realised he couldn't do anything about it, as the main tap was in Mr. Shew's basement, and he realised that if it went on it would soon bring somebody up. So he stowed the body in the cupboard and did a bolt. The water was spouting just outside the cupboard already, that's how his coat got wet. He must have got out of the house only just before Mrs. Haddow started looking into things. He went back to his office and fixed up with his partner and secretary to fake that alibi for him. The partner would have been as much affected as Boyle if they'd had to produce the money, and it seems the secretary's the partner's mistress. Together with the fact that Winters once paid attention to Wragge's wife, which Wragge was afraid to admit, he thought he'd got things all nice and safe. But he forgot that he'd picked up the loaf of bread. It was just one of those little automatic actions that so often give people away. It's those, as often as not, that tell you all you need to know about them."

"Well, I trust," Mr. Shew said, "and so, I'm sure, does Mrs. Haddow, that such a thing never happens again. D'you know, we haven't had a drop of water in the house for two days? Of course, we couldn't turn it on again until the pipe was mended, and that night it froze again and it's been frozen ever since. I don't know when we shall be able to lead a normal life. And my poor Miss Pattison's no better. Of course"—and he tittered—"it's really very amusing in some ways. Here am I, Chairman of the Baths and Cemeteries Committee, and I can't get a bath!"

"Perhaps you could get a coffin," Mr. Cust suggested, bunching all his features together and laughing through his fingers.

THE TRUTHFUL WITNESS

"Mrs. Nettle," the child said. "Mrs. Nettle—it's cold enough for snow, isn't it?"

The elderly woman, sitting in the armchair near the fire, went on with the swift darning of the grey sock stretched over her hand.

"I shouldn't wonder," she agreed.

"I think it's going to snow," the child said. "It is, isn't it, Mrs. Nettle?"

"I shouldn't be surprised," the woman said.

"When it snows, I'm going to make a snowman," the child said.

Snipping off an end of grey wool, the woman reached for another strand with which to re-thread her needle.

"You need a lot of snow for that," she said.

"Then I hope it snows and snows. I hope it snows all day and all night and all tomorrow and all the day after."

"Nasty messy stuff," the woman said. "Messy and cold and wet."

"But children like snow, don't they?" Turning from the window, the child came to lean on the arm of the old woman's chair. "Mrs. Nettle—they do, don't they, Mrs. Nettle?"

The corners of the woman's mouth twitched and she lowered her hands and her darning into her lap.

"That's right, love, they do. I should've remembered. All the same, don't you go bringing a lot of slush into the house on your boots, or I'll get after you, I can promise you."

With a deep sigh and her eyes fixed intently on the woman's, as if to extract a different promise, the child said, "I *hope* it starts soon."

"Well, if it doesn't, it'll come some other time, that's something you can be sure of. You've never seen snow, have you, living in Egypt?"

"No."

"And you're six years old."

"That isn't very old," the child said defensively. "There are lots of things I've never seen. I've never seen the Tower of London."

"There are lots of things I've never seen, and won't either," the woman said.

"Have you ever seen an elephant?"

The conversation continued beside the bright fire, while outside the afternoon sky darkened unnaturally early, looking as if it had grown so heavy that it might sink down to rest on the tops of the trees, and the trees bent and tossed their branches wildly, as if they were protesting at the threatened load, and the wind made strange wailing noises in the chimney.

A little before five o'clock the child's mother came home. She came running up the garden path, clutching her fur coat round her with one hand and holding on her little felt hat with the other. Her eyes and her cheeks were bright and her voice was high and gay. She too seemed to be almost bursting with excitement and desire at the thought of the snow. Yet on coming into the room, she said at once, "How cold and miserable it looks! Whyever haven't you drawn the curtains?"

"She wouldn't have it," Mrs. Nettle said, rising from the chair by the fire and beginning to roll up her mending. "She was afraid she'd miss the snow. It hasn't started yet, has it, Mrs. Ellis?"

The child was looking with some anxiety at the bright-cheeked young woman who was tugging the warm velvet curtains across the window.

"Mummy," she said "it *has* started, hasn't it, Mummy? On your coat! That's snow, isn't it? It is, isn't it?" Her voice was rising with each word.

"Yes, darling, it's just started." Her mother looked down at the small sequins of brightness that spangled the front of her coat. "It's nothing yet, but I shouldn't wonder if it's deep by tomorrow morning."

"How deep?"

"Oh, ever so deep."

"Enough to make a snowman?"

Mrs. Nettle had put her darning away in a cretonne bag. "If you don't mind, Mrs. Ellis," she said, "I think I'll be getting straight home. I'd sooner get home before the road gets slippery. I washed up the lunch things and I put all the tea things on the trolley. You've only to boil the kettle."

"Thank you, Mrs. Nettle, thank you so much." The young woman beat at her coat with her hands, so that the little drops of melting snow fell on the carpet. "It was so good of you to stay on. I hope Meg hasn't been too much trouble."

"No, I wasn't any trouble at all," the child said.

The women smiled at one another and Mrs. Ellis went on, "It's so nice to get out sometimes on one's own. I'm really grateful."

"Well, I'll be glad to do it any time, if I can manage it," Mrs. Nettle said. "Did you see a nice picture?"

"Picture?" the young woman said vaguely. She was watching the child, who had gone to the window and, dragging aside one curtain, was pressing her face to the glass.

"Mummy," Meg cried, "it isn't snowing! I can't see anything. I don't believe it's snowing, Mummy."

"That's because of the wind blowing so hard," her mother

said. "You'd see it on the other side of the house." She opened her bag to pay Mrs. Nettle what she owed her for sitting-in with the child. "Yes, it was a good film," she added, "really quite good. I enjoyed it."

"Mummy, I can see Mr. Ferguson's house from here," Meg said, rubbing at the mist that her own breath formed on the glass. "He's just turned out all his lights. D'you think he's going for a walk in the snow? D'you think perhaps he's coming over to see us?"

"I'm quite sure he isn't," her mother answered.

Something in her tone, some emphasis or roughness, made Mrs. Nettle lift her eyebrows for an instant. But she lowered them quickly, as if she did not really want to see what she might if she looked longer. Taking the three half-crowns with a murmur of thanks, she said, "Well, I'll see you in the morning, unless I can't get here. I don't care for slippery roads. Good night, Mrs. Ellis." Going to the door, she called to the child, "Good night, love."

But Meg was too absorbed in what she could see through the window, if she let the curtain fall behind her head, shutting out the light of the room, to answer.

In the distance, across the common, where she had picked the first blackberries that she had ever eaten, during the first weeks that she had spent in England, she could see the lights in Mrs. Nettle's son-in-law's cottage. Beside it, less brightly lit, was the cottage lived in by the Irish family, and next door to that, the cottage of Mr. Brookes, who sometimes came to help with the garden. But over to the right, where Mr. Ferguson's house stood, and where a few minutes before lights had been shining from half the windows in the house, there was only darkness. After all, Meg thought, he must have gone out to look at the snow.

She had a great curiosity about Mr. Ferguson. It was not that she liked him much, for whenever he came to the house, something very peculiar always happened in it, some deep alteration in its atmosphere that brought a sense of crisis, of things stirring under the surface, almost of peril. Yet he was a cheerful, friendly man who often gave her presents and who had told her how to make a snowman, suggesting that he and she should make one together.

She was not yet quite convinced, however, that snow was really falling. She could see that something was moving in the air, moving with a wavering lightness, like an old lacy shawl being shaken out by hands delicately careful of its fineness. But still she could see nothing unusual on the ground, no shimmer of whiteness, no crystalline glitter.

From her conversations with Mrs. Nettle, she remembered a technical term. "Mummy, I don't believe it's going to lay."

"Lie," her mother said.

"Well, I don't believe—" Meg stopped, because she heard her mother give a deep sigh. She came out from behind the curtain. "Don't you like snow either? Mrs. Nettle doesn't. She says—" She stopped again, because it was clear to her that her mother was not listening.

The child looked at her uneasily. It had happened again, the thing that was always happening these days. Her mother had taken off her coat and hat and was sitting in the armchair by the fire, pressing her hands tightly to her temples, holding back the hair from her face, which was drained of all its brightness. Her body, crouched crookedly in the chair, looked spent of all its energy and her eyes, peering deeply into the fire and far beyond it, were dull and empty.

The child resented the abrupt change. Her memory was still very short, yet it seemed to her that in a place called Alexandria, which she had already forgotten far more than she pretended, such sharp transitions as this from excitable gaiety to dreary and unexplained lassitude, had hardly ever occurred. She had lived

then, she believed, at the heart of a cheerful calm, with an atten-
tive and happy mother to look after her.

Moving restlessly about the room, Meg tried to draw some attention to herself by her fidgeting, but her mother did not even
look at her.

Presently Meg asked querulously, "Why hasn't Daddy come
home yet?"

"His train hasn't got in," her mother said.

"But it's late."

Her mother glanced at her wrist-watch. "No, it's only the
snow making it get dark early. All the same, it's time I was getting the tea." She stood up. She was frowning, but as she met
the child's gaze, she summoned up a smile. "Did you have a
nice afternoon with Mrs. Nettle?"

"Oh yes, she's an awfully nice person," Meg said, responding
eagerly.

"What did you do?"

"We talked."

"All the time?"

"Well, some of the time we played beggar-my-neighbour, and
then I drew a picture for her. Mummy, shall we play cards
now?"

"I'm going to get the tea," her mother said. "Why don't you
go upstairs to the landing window and see if you can see
Daddy's train come in?"

"Will you play cards with me after tea?"

"Just one game, if you like. But then off you go to bed."

"All right, but I hope it's a long game—a terrifically long one!"
She laughed and ran upstairs to look out of the landing window.

It had been her own discovery, on coming to live in this
house, and it had greatly raised its value in her eyes, that from
this window she could see the railway-line, about a quarter of a
mile away. Most of the other windows in the house faced in the

opposite direction, towards the common, which her parents, to her surprise, considered an asset. However, they had come to realise the virtue, particularly on rainy days, of having one window in their house from which it was possible to watch the trains go by.

The most exciting train of the day was naturally the train on which her father returned from his work in the nearby town, or rather, for the first few weeks, this train had been the one that Meg had been most eager to see arrive at the station. Recently, for some reason, she had found herself forgetting to watch for it. Her father's arrivals home had somehow changed their character and she no longer felt the same impatience and eagerness working up in her, as the day wore on, as she had at first. He had a way now, when he came home, of sitting watching her mother in a heavy silence, answering only absently and nervously when Meg tried to make him talk. Once or twice this had been so unbearable that she had started to scream in an agony of uncontrolled temper, which had had a peculiarly terrible result. No one had blamed her, no one had taken any notice of her, but her father, usually a very quiet and gentle man, had suddenly started to abuse her mother in hideous, bitter words, as if it were she who was kicking, crying and behaving disgracefully.

At last her mother had answered, "But it's all over—I've told you so again and again. Why can't you believe me?"

"Because I know you, I know what you are!" he had shouted.

"Then let's go away from here—far away—as far as you like! Will that convince you?"

"What's the good of going away?" he had asked. "Hasn't it always been the same, wherever we've been, except that you didn't let me know so much about it?"

"Sometimes I think you're crazy," her mother had said.

None of it made any sense to the child, but that scene was the most frightening thing that had ever happened to her, and some of the fear that she had felt then in the midst of her own helpless rage, was now projected on to the train that came snaking through the dusk every evening at five thirty-five, its windows all beautifully glowing.

But this evening she could not think seriously about anything but the snow, and she went upstairs happily to watch for the train. The snow made everything different. For one thing, as she saw as soon as she reached the landing, it had almost completely blocked the window and she was hardly able to see out at all. Great flakes were being hurled against the glass by the north wind. A drift had thickened already along the window-ledge. A white crust had formed round the edges of each pane and a fine spray seemed mysteriously to be coming straight through the glass itself and falling in tiny crystals on the sill inside.

Through the rapidly thickening curtain, Meg saw a flicker of lights outside in the darkness, telling her that her father's train was arriving, but it was the wonder of the snow itself that held her tense and still. Then suddenly, with a shrill squeal of excitement, she raced downstairs.

"Mummy, it's snowing right into the house!" she shrieked. "Mummy—"

As she reached the bottom of the stairs, the hall door opened. A freezing gust blew in from the garden and she saw an extraordinary figure standing there, a figure such as she had never seen before. It had a white hat, a white coat, queer bulky white boots and even bristling white eyebrows and a white moustache on an oddly grey-white face. Against the darkness it looked enormously tall. Quivering with shock at the surprise, it took the child a moment to recognise her father.

When that happened, she could not help shouting with laughter.

"I thought you were a snowman!" she cried. "You look just like a snowman!" Turning, she rushed on into the kitchen.

"Mummy, come and look—Daddy's come home and he looks just like a snowman!"

Her mother was toasting some bread under the grill. She put a hand over her eyes and said in a shaky, muffled voice, "For God's sake don't make such a row—it'll drive me mad!"

Too excited to take much notice of her mother's odd tone, the child ran back to the hall.

Her father was still in the open doorway, but he had turned his back on the house and was beating the snow off the front of his coat with his gloved hands and stamping his feet on the brick doorstep, so that the chunks of snow that had made his boots look so big fell away from them. When he turned again, coming in and closing the door and beginning to unbutton his wet, dark overcoat, he was no longer a strange, white, almost faceless monster, but was the familiar figure who always arrived home at this time.

The child ran ahead of him into the living-room, thinking that he would follow her at once, as he usually did, to warm himself at the fire. The room felt delightfully cosy after the cold and draughty landing, though the fire, which her mother had made up with fresh coal before going to make the tea, was not burning well.

Making a great show of warming her hands at it and of stamping her feet on the hearthrug, as she had just seen her father do on the doorstep, the child called out, "D'you know the snow's coming right in at the window upstairs, Daddy? But the window's tight shut. I looked and I know it is. Can snow come through glass, Daddy?"

There was no answer and she realised that he had not followed her into the room, but was still in the hall. Yet no sound of voices or of movement reached her from it, and what seemed suddenly stranger, no sound came to her either from the kitchen, where a moment before her mother had been moving quickly about, making the tea. The silence in the house was so complete that Meg might have been alone in it.

Instantly the swift panic of her age seized her and she felt utterly convinced that both of her parents had gone away and left her in an empty house in the midst of a terrible storm. She rushed to the door.

They were both there, just outside it, staring at one another across the small hall. The woman's eyes were enormous and terrified in her colourless face, the man's eyes burned feverishly. But there was something so alike in the expressions on their dissimilar faces that for once they bore a strange resemblance to one another. Both of them were shivering.

The woman was the first to speak.

"No!" she said hoarsely in answer, as even the child realised, to something that had not been said. Flinging up one arm, as if to keep something away from her, she repeated it, *"No!"*

The man raised his hands. He raised them only a few inches and looked at them as if he had never seen them before. They must be very cold, the child thought, they were shaking so.

"I didn't know I was going to—I swear to God I didn't. I didn't mean to, I didn't plan—but I had to know, I couldn't bear it any longer. So I came home early. I saw you together. But what happened after that . . ."

He stopped as the woman turned her head sharply to look at the child, standing in the doorway of the living-room.

More slowly he also turned his head and they both went on looking at her and the silence returned, a silence that made her start to shiver too, though it held her motionless, as though in the most evil of spells.

Mercifully her mother released her from it.

"Go back into the room, go back at once and shut the door," she said in a thin, jerky voice. "You'll catch cold out here."

Quietly the child turned and went back into the room.

She was glad to go, yet the room no longer seemed as warm as before, or as safe and pleasant. As she closed the door, which she did softly, with both hands on the big round doorknob, releasing it very carefully, fearing to contribute by the least heedlessness to the incomprehensible strain of the situation, she heard her mother say in an even stranger tone, "But what will you do now? What shall we—what can we do?"

Meg went to the fire and knelt down in front of it. The fresh, piled-up coal, which had hardly begun to burn, was like a rampart between her and the glowing heart of the fire. No flame, but only brown, acrid-smelling smoke streamed up the chimney. She felt disgusted with it. She knew that she was not allowed to touch it and at that moment she had no thought of doing so, but as the minutes passed and no one else came to tend the fire or to bring the tea, the silence and the bleakness of the room began to affect her like an active hostility. An overmastering desire came to her to do something drastic, violent. Grasping the poker, she snatched a quick glance over her shoulder at the closed door, then thrust the point deep into the fire.

At first nothing much happened, but when she had repeated the action two or three times, a little flame came licking up from under a piece of coal. Sitting back, she watched with absorption and saw a second little flame appear, and then another, and then two of them lean towards each other and play together, until, with a sudden roaring, they fused and shot upwards in a broad, yellow tongue of fire.

As the heat from it stung her cheeks, the child gave a wriggle of pleasure and withdrawing the poker, laid it down on the exact spot from which she had taken it up, so that no one could know that she had been playing with it. Entranced by the new life that she had stirred into being in the fireplace, she watched it with a hypnotized stare and hardly noticed when, a few minutes later, the door opened and her parents came in.

Her mother was pushing the tea-trolley, her father was smoking a cigarette. They went to their usual chairs on either side of the fireplace and her mother started to pour out the tea. For a little while Meg thought that everything had returned to normal, except that neither of them spoke at all. But this was not really so unusual nowadays that it worried her particularly. Then she noticed that when her mother handed her father his cup of tea, his hands were still shaking so much that he slopped half of it into the saucer.

"Are you very cold?" Meg asked solicitously. "Snow's always very cold, isn't it?"

"Yes," he said, "that's it, I'm cold." His voice was so low that she could hardly hear it.

"Perhaps you've caught a cold," she said. "When Mrs. Nettle's son-in-law had a cold he lost his voice. Are you losing your voice, d'you think?"

"Perhaps I am," he said.

"If you are," she said, "you won't be able to help me make a snowman tomorrow, will you?"

"Anyway, Daddy has to go to work tomorrow, as usual," her mother said. "I'll help you make a snowman."

It struck the child with faint surprise that work and other commonplace things should go on when there was snow on the ground.

"Mr. Ferguson said he'd help me make a snowman," she said.

Abruptly her father put down his plate, which had some hot buttered toast on it, and put his hands to his head.

"Jim!" his wife said warningly. She went on, "Yes, I'm sure Mr. Ferguson will help you. We'll go over in the morning and ask him."

The man made a queer, groaning sound. It distressed Meg, but she thought it might be best not to notice it.

"I think Mr. Ferguson likes snow," she said, "not like Mrs. Nettle. He went out for a walk when it started to snow."

"A walk!" her father cried. "Good God, what made you think—?"

"Jim!" his wife said again. "She saw his lights go out, that's all. *That's all*, do you hear?"

He drew several choking breaths.

"I can't go on with this," he muttered. "I can't go through with it. It's no good, Marion, I'll never be able to do it. I might as well give myself up right away. It'll be better for you both. I'll go. I'll go and tell them . . ." His voice died away.

The woman stooped over the child. "What a mess you're making with all that jam," she said. "Why can't you just eat it, instead of smearing it all over the plate?"

"I like looking at the pattern on the plate through it," Meg said. "It makes it look all pink."

"Well, that isn't good manners."

"Marion, for God's sake—what's the good of it?" the man whispered. "What hope is there?"

The woman straightened up again, looking at him, and one of those unspoken messages which, the child had noticed, were always passing between grown-up people, passed between them then. He reached for his wife's hand, clung to it, then started covering it with kisses.

"I don't know, I don't understand, why you're doing this for me—you of all people," he said. "I thought—when I came in tonight I thought—"

The woman gave a sigh and there was a soft, exhausted gentleness in her voice as she replied, "I don't understand it either. It just seems . . . Well, we'll talk about it later. All you need to remember now is that you came home on the usual train. And came straight home."

"Yes," he said, "the usual train."

"And after tea we're all going to play cards—just as usual."

"Beggar-my-neighbour!" the child cried. "All of us—Daddy too?"

Her mother nodded. "But one game only, remember, then off to bed with you and no fuss about it. Promise?"

The child promised eagerly. To have her father joining in the game, instead of hiding himself behind the evening newspaper, far from being usual, was an astonishing privilege, which she was more than ready to earn by going to bed in mouse-like silence. Yet even as she was giving her promise, she started asking herself how it was possible for her mother to believe that her father had returned from work on the usual train, when in fact he had been standing in the doorway of his home at the very time when the lights of his train could be seen going by from the window upstairs. That was a very puzzling thing to think about.

They played the one game of beggar-my-neighbour, which, luckily for the child, was a long one, then she obediently went upstairs. During the game her parents had both been quiet, neither of them responding at all when for a little while Meg had grown uproarious, and sometimes they had spoken to one another strangely. Yet there had been something in the way that they had looked at one another, and at her, which had made her feel that for that one evening they were all curiously at peace. It was a feeling that she had had too seldom lately, though she realised this only as it came to her again, reminding her of something past, something lost, and though she could not recall exactly when she had known it better, she recognised it instantly as sweetly, reassuringly familiar.

When she woke in the morning, she blinked in surprise at the brilliance of the light in her room. It was as dazzling as on a summer morning, though the brightness reflected on the ceiling over her bed had a tinge of blue in it that was not like summer sunshine.

Jumping out of bed, she ran to the window and saw, under a tranquil blue sky, the white covering on the garden and the common and on the bare branches of the trees. She saw too how the boughs of the evergreen bushes in the garden were weighed down by their load and how the path to the gate had quite disappeared.

As she looked, she saw her father come out of the house. He was wearing gum boots and a duffle-coat and was carrying a shovel, with which he started to clear the snow from the path. So, after all, he had not gone to the office. He dug fiercely, as if he were in a great hurry, yet in spite of this, he kept stopping and straightening his back to gaze across the common at Mr. Ferguson's house.

Mr. Ferguson, the child could see, had visitors. It seemed early in the day to be paying visits, yet a lot of people must have come to call on him, because there were several cars drawn up outside his house.

She had her breakfast alone with her mother, while her father went on working in the snow. Her mother looked very tired this morning. Her face seemed to have grown thin in the night, her fine, clear skin to have shrunk against the bone behind it.

"Isn't Daddy going to have any breakfast?" the child asked as she spooned up her porridge.

"He's had all he wants," her mother said.

"Isn't he going to the office?"

"Not yet."

"Isn't he well?"

"No—no, he isn't very well."

"Why doesn't he go to bed then?"

"He isn't ill enough for that."

The sound of the vacuum-cleaner, operated by Mrs. Nettle in one of the bedrooms, stopped abruptly and Mrs. Nettle's heavy footsteps came pounding down the stairs. She put her head into the dining-room.

"Looks as if some of them are coming here now, Mrs. Ellis," she said. "I saw them from the window."

The younger woman looked at her vacantly and said nothing.

"They'll be wanting to ask if you saw or heard anything, I suppose," Mrs. Nettle said, "like they did with us. He isn't bad, the inspector, he was quite polite. He won't worry you."

The child twisted in her chair to look out of the window and see who was coming, but she could not see beyond the laurel hedge.

Her mother got up, putting both hands on the table and leaning on them, as if her legs for a moment had become too weak to carry her, then she walked slowly out of the room. The child dropped her spoon and was going to jump off her chair and run after her, when Mrs. Nettle said sharply, "Now then, you get on with your breakfast and don't go sticking your nose into everyone's business."

"But, Mrs. Nettle, I want to know who it is," the child said.

"It's no one you know," Mrs. Nettle said, and went out and shut the door.

Meg waited for a moment, then she got down from her chair, walked softly across the room, turned the doorknob, quietly opened the door a few inches and peeped out.

Through the door opposite, which was wide open, she saw her father and mother in the garden, standing side by side on the cleared path, her mother's arm through her father's, while two men approached them from the gate. Listening eagerly, Meg heard her father say that it was a terrible thing that had happened, and her mother add that they had heard about it from the postman and had at once decided that her husband should stay at home that morning, in case he could give assistance of any kind. Then they all turned towards the house and the child, swiftly closing the dining-room door, ran back to her place at the table and went on hastily eating her cooling porridge.

A few minutes later Mrs. Nettle returned to the dining-room, bringing Meg a boiled egg. Unexpectedly she sat down at the table with her, watching her with a distressed and wondering stare, as if she had just become a problem about which the old woman had to make up her mind.

"Isn't Mummy going to finish her breakfast?" Meg asked presently.

"Yes, when the gentlemen have gone," Mrs. Nettle answered.

"What have they come for?"

"Now, didn't I tell you to mind your own business?"

Meg wriggled in exasperation. "But Daddy said something terrible's happened. What's happened, Mrs. Nettle?"

The old woman gave a sigh and said, "Well, for sure you'll hear about it, I suppose . . . There's been an accident, love."

"A motor accident?"

"No, a different kind of accident."

"In the snow? Did Mr. Ferguson fall down and hurt himself?" But before Mrs. Nettle could answer, Meg went on, "D'you know snow can blow straight through a window, even when it's shut? I didn't know that before, did you? I stood in front of the landing window and snow was blowing right into my face. I opened my mouth wide and the snow came into it and tasted just like ice-cream, only it didn't exactly taste at all. And the window was shut all the time."

"Oh, that window," Mrs. Nettle said. "It fits that badly, it always does that when there's a strong wind that side of the house. The snow wasn't coming through the glass."

"But I *saw* it, Mrs. Nettle."

"There's lots of things people think they see what they don't,"

Mrs. Nettle said, "and if they'd talk less about what they see, even when they *have* seen it, there'd be less damage done."

Before the child could puzzle this out, the door opened and her father, her mother and the two strange men came into the room.

Mrs. Nettle got to her feet, but instead of leaving the room, as Meg expected, she went to stand behind her, and in passing, she let her hand rest gently on Meg's shoulder. It was as if she thought the child needed reassurance and did not trust anyone else there to give it to her.

Meg's mother spoke to her. "This gentleman wants to ask you something, darling. He thinks perhaps you can tell him something he wants to know."

Angrily Mrs. Nettle exclaimed, "How can she tell him anything? She doesn't even understand—"

"Please," Meg's father said. He lifted a hand to check her.

"She can answer this question, I'm sure," one of the strange men said, smiling at the child as he came towards her. His breath smelt strongly of tobacco. He was a very big man, with smooth ruddy skin and grey hair.

"It's a very easy question," he said, "nothing to worry about at all. You don't mind answering it, do you, my dear?"

She looked at her mother, then at her father, then back at the big man.

"No," she said uncertainly.

"Well now, you remember you were in the other room yesterday afternoon, and you went to look out of the window?"

"Yes."

"What did you see?"

She again searched the faces of everyone else in the room before she committed herself to an answer.

"The snow," she said.

"Ah," he said, "the snow. You like snow, eh?"

"I—I don't know."

"Now, that's queer, a little girl not knowing what she likes and what she doesn't," he said. "Most of the little girls I know, know much too much about it."

"But I never saw snow before in my whole life," she explained.

"Well, well!" he said. "So you were very excited, I expect. And you went to the window to watch the snow falling."

"Yes."

"And what else did you see?"

She returned his steady, smiling look warily. She knew at once that this was the question that he really wanted answered and that the other questions about the snow had not meant anything. But this knowledge confused her, so that she could not remember anything at all of what she had seen from the window.

At length she said, "I didn't see anything."

"What, nothing at all?"

"Just tell the inspector what you told me," her mother prompted her. "Don't you remember what you told me you saw?"

Breathing heavily, Meg screwed up her forehead and twisted about in her chair.

"I saw the lights in Mr. Ferguson's house," she said.

"The lights? Yes, and then?" the big man asked.

"I saw them go out and I said—I said to Mummy, Mr. Ferguson's going for a walk in the snow."

"That's fine, that's just fine," he said. "Now, I don't suppose you could help me a lot more by telling me when this happened."

Her mother answered for her, "I'm afraid she isn't very good at telling the time yet, Inspector. But Mrs. Nettle might be able to tell you that."

He looked up at the old woman. "You were here?"

"I was," she said sourly.

"And do you know what time it was when the little girl saw the lights go out?"

"Is that when—when it happened?" she asked.

"Seems likely," he said. "Most of the curtains weren't drawn, only the bedroom curtains, and he must have been afraid someone could see in."

"Well, it was about five then, because it was just before I went home," Mrs. Nettle said, "and I got home about quarter past."

"Thanks," he said. "Thanks very much." He looked round and addressed them all. "I'm sorry to have troubled you, but you understand we have to ask these questions. And we'll have to corroborate that you came home on the five-thirty, Mr. Ellis, as you said. That's just routine, of course."

The child's parents nodded silently.

The big man looked down at the child.

"I expect you saw your father come home, didn't you, young lady? But you wouldn't know just when it was, if you aren't very clever at telling the time yet."

"Oh, I do," she said.

She looked up into her father's face as she said it. Even before she saw the sudden panic in his eyes, she knew that she was on dangerous ground. But she had confidence in herself, because, although she had not understood it at the time, she had learnt her lesson well the evening before, and she knew that she could repeat it accurately.

"I know just when it was," she said, "because I saw his train come in. I watched it from the landing window, like I always do —well, almost always. And then—then—" She choked with the effort to be clear, to make no mistake. Apart from her own high voice, stumbling on, there was an extraordinary silence in the room. "Then of course he came home, like he always does, and I—I met him at the door. And he came in looking like a snowman!"

With the last sentence she burst out laughing. This was not only because she had suddenly remembered vividly how funny it had been not to recognise her father, and actually be frightened of him. More than that, it was because of the relief of being able to tell the easy truth again, instead of the incomprehensible, memorized lie.

The big man smiled at her again. "A snowman?" he said.

"Yes, he had snow on his eyebrows and his moustache and all down him," she said.

"That must have looked funny." He turned towards the door.

The child's father, smiling a little himself, though his manner was very grave, followed him out of the room and opened the front door. Beyond it, in the garden, the snow glittered in the calm, brilliant sunshine.

The big man turned up the collar of his coat. "She'll have a fine time, mucking about with the first snow she's seen in her long life, eh? And it's fine and dry for her too, now that that wind's dropped . . ." He paused. For a moment his face looked oddly empty and stupid, as if he had had a shock. "That north wind . . . And you came in looking like a snowman, Mr. Ellis? But if you'd been coming from the station in that north wind, you'd have had the snow behind you and you wouldn't have looked like a snowman to your daughter till you turned your back on her. You'd have looked like a snowman only if you'd been coming in the opposite direction—*from across the common,* Mr. Ellis! And it could be, after all, that there's more truth than you've both been telling me in those stories I've heard about your wife and Mr. Ferguson."

The child saw her father sway where he stood. She heard her mother scream. Then she felt Mrs. Nettle's arms about her and found her face firmly held against Mrs. Nettle's bosom, so that she could not see what else was happening. Everyone in the hall seemed to be talking or shouting at the same time, while Mrs. Nettle bore Meg away to the kitchen, muttering in her ear, "God help you, my poor love, God help you!"

GO, LOVELY ROSE

It was on the day that Mrs. Holroyd refused Mr. Pocock's offer of marriage that he first thought of murdering her. The rejection, so gently and kindly put, but so utterly unexpected, filled him first with astonishment, so that he felt as if he had tripped over something uneven in his path and fallen flat on his face, and then with a searing rage. For a wild moment he wanted to clasp his hands round her slender neck and squeeze the life out of her. But after that flare of hatred came fear. He had made up his mind, after his last murder, never to kill again.

On that occasion he had escaped arrest only by the skin of his teeth and he knew that the police still believed that he was guilty, although they had never had enough evidence to bring a charge against him. That had been largely due to Lucille's passion for cleanliness. She had polished and washed and scrubbed everything in her little flat at least twice a week, so that the police, in their investigation, had not been able to find a single one of Mr. Pocock's fingerprints. Dear Lucille. He remembered her still with a kind of affection, partly because she had co-operated so beautifully in her own death. Except, of course, for that business of the roses. It was that love that she had had for roses and the pleasure that it had given him to bring them to her from his own little garden that had almost destroyed him.

There had been no complications like that about his first murder. Almost no drama either. He had nearly forgotten why he had committed it. Alice had been a very dull woman. He could hardly recollect her features. However, it had happened one day that she had told him in her flat, positive way that she did not believe a word that he had told her about his past life, that she was sure that he had never been an intelligence officer during the war, that he had never been parachuted into occupied France, that he had never been a prisoner of the Nazis and survived hideous tortures at their hands, in all of which she had been perfectly correct, and really the matter had been of very little importance, but her refusal to share his fantasies had seemed to him such a gross insult that for a few minutes it had felt impossible to allow her to go on living. Afterwards he had walked quietly out of the house, it turned out that no one had seen him come or go, and her death had become one of the unsolved mysteries in the police files. There had been a certain flatness about it, almost of disappointment.

But in Lucille's case it had been quite different. For one thing, he had been rather fond of her. She had been an easy-going woman, comfortable to be with, and she had never expected gifts other than the flowers that he brought her. But one day when he had happened to say how much he wished that she could see them growing in his glowing flower-beds, but that the anxious eye of his invalid wife, who would suffer intensely if she even knew of Lucille's existence, made this impossible, she had gone into fits of laughter. She had told him that there was no need for him to tell a yarn like that to her of all people, and he had realised all of a sudden that she had never believed in the existence of any frail, lovely, dependent wife to whom he offered up the treasures of his loyalty and charity. The dangerous rage that had possessed him only a few times in his life exploded like fireworks in his brain. It had seemed to him that she was mocking him not merely for having told her lies that had never deceived her, but for having tried to convince her that any woman, even a poor invalid, could ever love him enough to marry him. His hands, made strong by his gardening, although they were small and white, had closed on her neck, and when he left her she had been dead.

By chance he had left no fingerprints in her flat that day. But he had been seen arriving by the woman who lived in the flat below Lucille's. Meeting on the stairs on his way up, he and the woman, an elderly person in spectacles, had even exchanged remarks about the weather, and it turned out that she had taken particular notice of the bunch of exquisite Kronenbourgs that he had been carrying. The rich velvety crimson of the blooms and the soft gold of the undersides of the petals and their delicious fragrance had riveted her attention, a fact which at first he had thought would mean disaster for him, but which actually had been extraordinarily fortunate. For afterwards she had been able to describe the roses minutely, but had given a most inaccurate description of the man who had been carrying them, and in the identity parade in which he had been compelled to take part when the police had been led to him by a telephone number scrawled on a pad in Lucille's flat, the woman had picked out the wrong man. So the police had had no evidence against him except for the telephone number and the rosebush in his garden. But half a dozen of his neighbours, who had imitated him when they had seen the beauty of that particular variety of rose, had Kronenbourgs in their gardens too, and so Lucille's murder, like Alice's, had remained an unsolved mystery.

Yet not to the police. Mr. Pocock was sure of that and sometimes the thought that he might somehow betray himself to them, even now after two years, that he might drop some word or perform some thoughtless action, though heaven knew what could do him any damage after all his time, made terror stab him like a knife. He would never kill again, of that he was certain.

But that was before Mrs. Holroyd refused to marry him.

It had taken a long time to convince himself that marriage to

her would be a sound proposition, even though he was certain
that she had been pursuing him ever since she had come to live
in the little house next to his. She was a widow and she believed
him to be a widower, and she often spoke to him of her loneliness since her husband's sudden death and sympathised with
Mr. Pocock because of his solitary state. She admired his garden
and took his advice about how to lay out her own, was delighted
with the gifts of flowers that he brought her, and when he was
ill with influenza she did his shopping for him, cooked him
tempting little meals and changed his books at the library. And
she had let him know, without overstressing it, that her income
was ample.

"I'm not a rich woman," she had said, "but thanks to the
thoughtfulness of my dear husband, I have no financial worries."

So it seemed clear to Mr. Pocock that Mrs. Holroyd's feelings
were not in doubt and that it was only his own that it was necessary for him to consider. Did he want marriage? Would he be
able to endure the continuous company of another person after
all his years of comfortable solitude? Would not the effort of
adapting his habits to fit those of someone else be an extreme irritation? Against that, he was ageing and that bout of influenza
had shown him how necessary it was to have someone to look
after him. And marrying Mrs. Holroyd might actually be finan-
cially advantageous instead of very expensive, as it would be to
employ a housekeeper. She was a good-looking woman too, for
her age, and an excellent cook. If he wanted a wife, he could
hardly do better.

Of course, she had certain little ways that he found very hard
to tolerate. She liked to sing when she was doing her housework.
If he had to listen to it in his own house, instead of softened by
distance, it would drive him mad. She chatted to all the neighbours, instead of maintaining a courteous aloofness, as he did.
She had a passion for plastic flowers. Every vase in her house

was filled with them, with a total disregard for the seasons, her tulips and daffodils blooming in September and her chrysanthemums in May. She always thanked him with a charming lighting up of her face for the flowers that he brought her, but he was not really convinced that she could distinguish the living ones from the lifeless imitations. But no doubt, with tact, he would be able to correct these small flaws in her. On a bright evening in June, he asked her to marry him.

She answered, "Oh, dear Mr. Pocock, how can I possibly tell you what I feel? I am so touched, so very honoured! But I could never marry again. It would not be fair to you if I did, for I could never give my heart to anyone but my poor Harold. And our friendship, just as it is, is so very precious to me. I think we are wonderfully fortunate, at our age, to have found such a friendship. To change anything about it might only spoil it. So let us treasure what we have, won't that be wisest? What could we possibly give to each other more than we already do?"

He took it with dignity and accepted a glass of sherry from her. What made the occasion particularly excruciating for him was his certainty that she had known that he was going to propose marriage and had had her little speech all ready rehearsed. It disgusted him to discover that all her little kindnesses to him had simply been little kindnesses that had come from the warmth of her heart and not from any desire to take possession of him. Looking at her, with her excellent sherry tasting like acid in his mouth, he was suddenly aware of the terrible rage and hatred that he had not felt for so long. However, he managed to pat her on the shoulder, say that of course nothing between them need be altered, and go quietly home.

The most important thing for the moment, it seemed clear to him, was not to let her guess what her refusal had done to him. She must never be allowed to know what power she had to hurt him. Everything must appear to be as it had been in the past. In fact, their relationship was poisoned for ever, but to save his pride this must be utterly hidden from her. Two days later he appeared on her doorstep, smiling, and with a beautiful bunch of Kronenbourgs for her.

She exclaimed over them with extra special gladness and there was a tenderness on her face that he had never seen there before. She was so happy, he thought, to have humiliated him at apparently so little cost to herself. Tipping some plastic irises and sprays of forsythia out of one of the vases in her sitting-room, she went out to the kitchen to fill the vase with water, brought it back and began to arrange the roses in it.

Up to that moment he had not really intended to murder her. He would find some way of making her suffer as she was making him suffer, but when his hands went out to grasp her neck and he saw at first the blank astonishment on her face before it changed to terror, he was almost as surprised and terror-stricken as she was. When she fell to the floor at his feet in a limp heap and he fled to the door, he was shaking all over.

But then he remembered something. The Kronenbourgs. Once before they had almost destroyed him. This time he would not forget them and leave them behind. Turning back into the room, he snatched the roses from the vase, jammed the plastic flowers back into it, and only pausing for a moment at the front door to make sure that the street was empty, made for his own home. Inside, he threw the roses from him as if they carried some horrible contagion and for some time left them lying where they had fallen, unable to make himself touch them. How mad he had been to take them to the woman! How easily fatal to him they could have been! He drank some whisky and smoked several cigarettes before he could force himself to pick them up and put them in a silver bowl, which he stood on a bookcase in his sitting-room. They looked quite normal there, not in the least like witnesses against him. It was very important that everything should look normal.

Next morning, when two policemen called on him, he was of course prepared for them and felt sure that his own behaviour was quite normal. But he was worried by a feeling that he had met one of them before. The man was a superintendent who told him that the body of his neighbour, Mrs. Holroyd, had been discovered by her daily woman, choked to death, then went on to ask him when he had seen her last and where he had spent the evening. He supposed that such questions were inevitable, but he did not like the way, almost mocking, that the man looked at him.

Then, standing looking at the roses in the silver bowl, the superintendent remarked admiringly, "Lovely! Kronenbourgs, aren't they?"

"Yes," Mr. Pocock said, "from my garden."

"I've got some in my own garden," the superintendent said. "There's nothing to compare with a nice rose, is there? Now, your neighbour doesn't seem to have cared for flowers. She stuck to the plastic kind. Less trouble, of course. But a funny thing about her, d'you know, she kept some of them in water? Some irises and forsythia, they were in a vase full of water, just as if they were real. That's carrying pretence a bit far, wouldn't you say, Mr. Pocock? Unless there'd been some real flowers there first, like, say, your roses. You'd a way of giving her flowers, hadn't you, Mr. Pocock? That's something she told the neighbours. But really you ought to have learnt better by now than to take them with you when you're going out to do your murders."

DRAWN INTO ERROR

Rina Evitt's eyes were stretched wide with fear. Staring across the room at her husband, they were not quite focussed.

"It'll never work," she said shrilly.

"It'll have to." Harry Evitt's voice was as empty of feeling as hers was charged with it. His nervousness was in his feet. With one heel he was trying to kick a hole in the costly grey rug before the fire. "Yes, it'll have to," he said without excitement, without doubt, without eagerness.

Rina dropped her head into her hands. Her hair tumbled over them as her fingers clawed her bursting temples. She had thick, bleached hair, with a sheen that was bright but lifeless. Her face was long, with slackly handsome features and big, wide-spaced eyes.

"I'll make a mess of it—there isn't time—there's too much to remember."

Knowing what she could do when she tried, her husband was not much troubled.

"You'll remember all right," he said. "It's just the timing that matters. The rest's easy. But make sure you get the timing right."

He shifted his weight from one foot to the other, dug the back of one heel into a new patch of rug and gave a fierce twist to his foot. A faint dent remained in the springy pile for a moment.

"You've got to be sure the others leave on time," he said.

"And you've got to be sure you get Minnie out into the drive with them, to see them off, so that you can come back in here and change the clock and make that telephone call without her knowing. And you've got to time that exactly. But the rest of it's easy."

Rina jerked her head up, staring at him again.

He was a man of middle height, softly covered in flesh, dressed in a dark grey suit, a white shirt, a dark blue tie, all good, all inconspicuous. He had a round, white face, moulded into features as insignificant as the dent that he had made in the carpet, and with thinning dark hair brushed back from a low, curved forehead.

With her eyes on that calm, dull face, Rina said, "You haven't just thought of this, Harry—not just today. You've had it ready for a long time, in case George ever found out about the money."

"All right, I've had it ready," Evitt said. "And a good thing I did, I'd say."

"You've had it ready, yet you never told me . . ."

"You know that's what I'm like," he said. "You ought to be used to it by now."

She swayed her head from side to side, not quite shaking it, not quite nodding. Crouched in her chair, shrunk into herself, she looked small, helpless and harmless. In fact, she was a tall woman, thin, but big-boned and strong.

"I'm not used to it," she said. "I never shall be."

Evitt's pale pink lips twitched at the corners in a faint expression of satisfaction. But life never remained long in his face.

"Remember—get them all out into the drive," he said, coaching her again with patience, with understanding, but with relentlessness. "Then run in and change the clock and make the telephone call. Make sure Minnie stays outside long enough for you to do that. Get her worrying about the roses. Or fertilizers. Anything. You can handle her."

"But the other part of it," Rina said. "Suppose *that* doesn't work."

"It will."

"No, it's too difficult, it's too complicated, there are too many things to go wrong." Her voice had leapt again into shrillness.

After a short silence, Evitt answered evenly, "All right then, what do we do instead?"

When she did not answer, he said, "Go and get changed now, Rina. Put on your green dress. Get the room ready. There isn't much time to spare."

She looked round dazedly. "The room's all right, isn't it? Just as usual."

"The room's fine." His pride in the room escaped into his voice for a moment.

It was a room of which they were both proud. The floor was of mahogany woodblocks. The picture window showed them a sweep of lawn, some early daffodils blooming in rough grass under bare trees, only distant roofs and still more distant hills. The antique furniture had been bought after careful study of the best magazines. There was excellent central heating.

"The tea's all ready," Rina said. "I've just got to get out the bridge-table and the cards."

"Get them out then," Evitt said. "Keep busy. Don't sit and think. It won't help you."

"And you . . . ?"

He walked over to her. He put his hands under her elbows and hauled her out of her chair.

"Don't think about me either."

She was slightly the taller of them, even without her high heels. Face to face with him now, she could look over his head to the window, to the cluster of leafless trees and the grey-green line of the low hills beyond them.

"You can do it, Rina," he said, his hands tight on her arms.

"I suppose I can," she said, "but I don't like it."

"Do you think I like it?"

He did not like it. He was terrified of what he had to do and of what might result from it for himself and for Rina. He was a calculating rather than a violent man. But calculations can go wrong, and when they do, what is there left but violence?

Rina's bridge-party broke up at six o'clock. It always did. Two of the four women who met every Wednesday to play had to catch a bus home from the end of the road at ten minutes past six. So when the hands of the grandfather clock in the corner of the room pointed to ten minutes to six, the losers groped in their handbags, paid out what they owed to the winners, re-hashed the blunders and disasters of the last rubber and made peace with each other.

"Not my lucky afternoon," Minnie Hobday said in a tone of unusual heaviness. She smoothed back one of her straying locks of grey hair, but left others, disturbed by the high wind of play, to droop around her square, mild face and support its gentle, sheep-dog quality. "I'm getting too old for this game."

Rina, sitting on her left, scribbling on a scoring-pad before her, tapped Minnie on the wrist with her pencil, a gesture that Rina seemed to be fond of. The pencil was of emerald green, tipped with gilt, and matched the emerald green woollen dress and the heavy gold bracelet that she was wearing.

"It isn't age that's the trouble," she said, smiling. "You've got something on your mind, Minnie."

"No, it's just age," Minnie Hobday said insistently. "I never had much of a memory for cards, and soon I suppose I shan't have any at all."

But the truth was that she had a great deal on her mind, that she was very worried, because for the last three days her husband, George, had barely spoken to her, and today he had gone to London without telling her the reason, all of which was quite unlike him.

Even if Minnie had reached the stage of wanting to confide in someone the terrible suspicion that had been torturing her all day, the suspicion that George was not well, that he had symptoms so fearful that he had not been able to bring himself to tell her about them, but had gone off alone to London to consult a specialist, it would never have occurred to her to confide in Rina Evitt. Though the two women had never had a quarrel, and during the five years since Rina's marriage to George's partner in the firm of Hobday and Hobday, auctioneers and estate agents, had made a habit of these weekly bridge afternoons, and of performing all sorts of small neighbourly acts for one another, Minnie had never even begun to grow intimate with the younger woman.

She was sorry for this. It would have been far better for all of them if she and Rina had been able to become as friendly as George was with Harry. But Rina, so Minnie, blaming herself, explained it, was young, was smart, had travelled, and apparently, in other places, had known really interesting people. So she could hardly be expected, could she, to be anything but bored by Minnie Hobday?

Minnie had always been aware of the boredom in Rina, of the emptiness, of the need for something more than she had. It was Minnie's belief that it would always be for more and more. Whatever Rina had would never be enough. Still, it had been clever of her to realise that Minnie had something on her mind. Ordinarily she seemed so wrapped up in herself, so like a child in a daydream, that you would no more expect her to notice a shade of worry on an elderly face than, come to think of it, you would expect her, all of a sudden, to be interested in the names of two undistinguished shrubs, growing near the gate, and which had been growing there for years.

So perhaps something was happening to Rina, some change, some development. That would be nice, Minnie thought, walking out to the gate with the other two women, and identifying the shrubs as a *laurustinus* and a *hypericum uralum*. But turning to Rina to tell her this, Minnie found that she had just gone back into the house.

Minnie did not leave then, for George had said that he would call for her on his way home from the station, and Rina was expecting her to wait for him. Returning to the house, Minnie found her setting a tray with a decanter of sherry and four glasses on it on a low coffee-table.

"I didn't see why we should wait for the men," Rina said. "A drink is what you need to cheer you up a bit. I suppose it's Michael you're worrying about, but you shouldn't, you know. He's all right, that boy."

Michael was the Hobdays' son, and because of a certain carelessness that he had sometimes shown in the handling of a fast car, he had more than once given his parents cause to worry about him. But recently he had been almost sensible.

"No, I'm not worried about Michael," Minnie said. "Really, I'm not worried about anything." She took the glass that Rina held out to her and glanced at the clock. George should be here at any moment, she thought. The suspense of the long day would soon be over.

However, it was not as late as she had thought that it must be, or so she believed until, a minute or two later, she happened to glance at her watch.

In surprise, she exclaimed, "That clock's wrong, Rina!"

"Not *that* clock," Rina said.

"It is, it's ten minutes slow," Minnie said. "George ought to be here."

Rina shook her head. There was a smile in her wide-spaced, candid eyes. "It's the most reliable thing on earth, Minnie, and so it should be, considering what care Harry takes of it—and what he paid for it."

"But this watch of mine is quite reliable too. I've had it for twenty-two years, and I never have to adjust it more than about two minutes in a month." Because of her worry, Minnie sounded querulous. "It's a very good watch."

Rina turned to the fire. She stirred the smouldering logs with the toe of her shoe. Her pale hair, swinging forward, hid her face.

"Perhaps it needs cleaning," she said.

"I had it cleaned two months ago. No, I'm sure it's the clock that's wrong. George ought to be here . . ." The sound of strain in her own voice checked Minnie.

"All right," Rina said equably. "I'll tell Harry. But talking of Michael, he's a crazy thing, but really so nice. Everyone thinks so. And even if he and George do get across one another, you shouldn't make up your mind it's all Michael's fault."

Frowning vaguely, Minnie wondered why Rina kept dragging Michael in. "I don't know what you mean about him and George getting across one another," she said. "They're ever such good friends nowadays. Of course, Michael went through a difficult phase. All boys do." She stopped, because she thought that she had heard footsteps outside on the gravel of the drive.

Rina had heard them too. "There's Harry," she said.

"Or George." Relying on her watch rather than on the Evitts' clock, Minnie believed that his train must have reached the station about ten minutes ago, and she knew that by the shortcut across the fields, he needed only five minutes to reach the Evitts' house.

"Yes—or George," Rina said, and went quickly out of the room.

Nervous and impatient, thinking of the dire news that he might be bringing her, Minnie made one of her random selections of an untidy lock of hair and smoothed it back from her forehead. At the same time she did her best to arrange a placid smile on her face. But it was Harry Evitt, not George, who received the smile.

"Ah, Minnie!" he said with evident pleasure.

"Good evening, Harry," she said. "You haven't seen George, I suppose? He was going to call in for me."

Evitt looked at the clock.

"Wasn't he coming on the six-twenty? That's only just due now."

"But that clock's slow," Minnie said. "It's half past six."

"*That* clock isn't slow," Evitt said, almost as Rina had said before him.

In a shriller voice, as if it mattered which was wrong, the Evitts' clock or her watch, Minnie said, "Well, by my watch it's half past six already. George ought to be here. He said he was going to come straight here from the station and not go to the office."

The Evitts exchanged glances.

"Well, let's check it on the telephone," Harry Evitt said. "You may be quite right, Minnie. If you are, I expect it's just that the train's late, but if you like I'll walk to the station and make sure . . . make sure . . ." He stopped, as if he were uncertain of what, in the circumstances, he ought to make sure.

Rina had already gone to the telephone. She picked it up, spoke into it and put it down again.

"The operator says it's six twenty-one by the clock in the exchange," she said, and picking up the glass of sherry that she had left behind when she had gone out to meet her husband, she drank it down and began to choke.

Evitt hit her between the shoulders. The sound of his hand, striking her, was surprisingly loud.

Wiping moisture from her eyes, Rina said hoarsely, "It's really Michael Minnie's worried about. That row they had."

"That was nothing," Evitt said. "Nothing at all. Have some more sherry, Minnie. George'll soon be here."

But even an hour later, George had not arrived at the Evitts' house.

The Evitts said that he must be coming on a later train. Minnie agreed with them and decided not to wait for him any longer. Evitt saw her down the short lane to her home. He went with her as far as her gate, then walked off into the darkness, while Minnie walked up the path to the door, a door set in a jutting Victorian porch and opening into a roomy but drably papered hall, across which an electric clock faced her, whirring softly. Comparing her watch with the clock, she saw that her watch was fast, but only by three minutes.

That was at seven-forty.

At seven fifty-five the police arrived. George had not come home by a later train. He had returned from London, as he had said that he would, on the six-twenty. The ticket-collector quite clearly remembered his handing in his ticket. Then George had started to walk across the fields to the Evitts' house.

At the time when his body was discovered, under a hedge with his head battered in, he had been dead for at least an hour.

Detective Superintendent Ronald Tewson was very interested in Minnie's watch. Had she or had she not re-set it at the Evitts' when she found that it and their clock did not agree? But Minnie by then was not in a state to give him an answer on which he could place much reliance.

At first, in her grief, she had maintained a dreadful, vacant composure. She had told the police all that she could, but had grown quietly more and more dazed and incoherent, till her son Michael, a tall boy of nineteen, who had been summoned from a cinema, had led her upstairs to her room and the doctor had given her an injection.

As he watched her go, not losing her gentle restraint, but only her mind, Tewson, who could almost deceive himself that he could take murder in his stride, felt something in himself that he dreaded, the sense of pressure, almost of blockage in his head, caused, as he knew, by extreme anger. For this, he was certain already, was a cold-blooded crime, and of all kinds of crimes, that was the kind that made his own blood the hottest. But with that anger in him he always wore himself out, suffered more than was useful to anyone, and jumped to unwarranted conclusions. The unwarranted conclusion to which he jumped before the night's work was over was that George Hobday had been murdered by his partner, Harry Evitt. All that funny business about the clock and the telephone call to the exchange. It was too convenient. But Tewson was not going to have anyone else saying anything of the sort yet.

"We haven't a thing against Evitt at the moment," he said dourly to Sergeant James Geary at one o'clock in the morning, as the two men gulped tea in Tewson's office. "That's the fact. Not a solid thing except that Mrs. Hobday doesn't think she re-set her watch before she got home. Doesn't *think* so! A solid fact, d'you call that?"

Geary was a younger, heartier man than Tewson.

"Look," he said, "it's the telephone call that's the only trouble, isn't it? The fact that they've confirmed it at the exchange that Mrs. Evitt did ring up and ask the time at six twenty-one, which made the Evitts' clock right and Mrs. Hobday's watch wrong, and put Evitt right there in the room with Mrs. Hobday when Hobday's train got in, and for an hour afterwards. That's all that's worrying you, isn't it?"

Tewson wagged his head in a furious parody of a nod of agreement.

"Of course a little thing like motive doesn't worry me," he said, his lips drawn back in a tight, ugly smile.

"You'll find that in the books of the company, I shouldn't wonder," Geary said. "There's been talk around for some time about where Evitt's getting his money from. When you've talked to that accountant Hobday went to see in London . . ."

"Go on and teach me my job," Tewson said. "It's that telephone call you're going to put me right on, isn't it?"

"There were two telephone calls," Geary said.

"That's right," Tewson said, "there probably were. One to the exchange and one to nowhere, and the one Mrs. Hobday heard was the one to nowhere. It could have been like that. Only if it was, I don't like it."

Geary looked faintly disappointed that his thinking had already been done for him.

"Why not?" he asked. "It's nice and simple."

"Simple!" Tewson said, as if the mere sound of the word made him feel ill.

"Look," Geary said, "they arrive for the bridge-party—Mrs. Hobday and the two other women—and they play for a couple of hours. All three have got watches, but not one of them says anything then about the clock being slow. And the party breaks up at the usual time, because two of them have to catch a bus. And they all go out in the garden together to see the two ladies off, and Mrs. Hobday also goes to look at some shrubs, because Mrs. Evitt's suddenly got interested in knowing what they are. But for some reason, instead of staying with Mrs. Hobday while she's looking at the shrubs, Mrs. Evitt doubles back into the house, and when Mrs. Hobday follows her, she's setting out drinks in the sitting-room. But by then Mrs. Evitt's had three or four minutes to herself, and that would be plenty of time to ring up the exchange, get told that the time was six twenty-one, then put the hands of the clock back to six-ten. Well then, presently Evitt comes in. It's really six-thirty, and he's met Hobday at the station, started across the fields with him, done him in and gone on home. But the clock says it's only six-twenty, and when Mrs. Hobday says the clock's wrong, they make a fake call to the exchange which convinces the old lady for the time being that her watch is wrong. Now, what's the matter with that?"

"Only that her watch wasn't wrong when she got home," Tewson said, "or only three minutes wrong, which doesn't signify. Or"—he rubbed the side of his jaw thoughtfully—"or does it?"

"But it's her watch not being wrong that proves all this," Geary said.

Tewson gave a weary shake of his head. "Evitt—a man like Evitt—he'd have thought of that, Jim. But when we saw him, he wasn't scared. Things had worked out just as he meant them to. So he's got something else up his sleeve, and that means there's something else coming, something for us to trip over and send us flat on our faces. Yes . . ." Tewson stopped as the telephone rang at his elbow, then, as he reached for it, repeated sombrely, "Yes, something else is coming."

His conversation on the telephone lasted for some minutes. When it was over, he looked expressionlessly at Geary, then leant back in his chair, stared up at the dingy ceiling and muttered, "Didn't I say?"

"What was it?" Geary asked.

"That was young Hobday," Tewson said. "His mother's watch is thirty-five minutes fast. In about six hours, it's gained nearly half an hour. What do you make of that, Jim?"

In disgust, Geary exclaimed, "That means her watch *was*

wrong at the Evitts'. She must have re-set it there and forgotten doing it. And it had already gained another three minutes by the time she got home. It's hopelessly out of order. Or did anyone get a chance to tamper with the watch?"

"The boy says not. He says she talked to him quite sensibly for a little while when he got her alone before the injection hit her, and she was quite sure no one had had a chance to tamper with it."

"Then you aren't going to be able to smash Evitt's alibi so easily."

"Because of the sheer coincidence that her watch, her good watch, that she's had for twenty-two years, went wrong the same evening as her husband was murdered?" Still staring at the ceiling, on to which, at one time or another, he had projected most of his problems, Tewson shook his head. "No," he said definitely.

"Then someone did tamper with it—stands to reason," Geary said.

"Yes."

"The boy?"

"Why?"

"Working with Evitt, perhaps. There's this story that he was on bad terms with his father."

"The Evitts' story. No one else supports it."

"But then . . ." Geary found himself staring at the ceiling. But he was unable to draw from it the inspiration that Tewson seemed to find there. Once more he fixed his eyes on Tewson's face, which just now was almost as grey, as lined and as blank as the ceiling.

"But then no one but Mrs. Hobday could have tampered with the watch," Geary said. "Mrs. Hobday herself. Only why should she do it? She seemed fond of her old man. So why should she do that to protect Evitt?"

"Just let me think, Jim," Tewson answered quietly. "Just let me think a little."

In the morning Harry Evitt did not go to the office. He knew that this was a mistake, but he was afraid to leave Rina by herself. The day before she had done her part well. Both in the handling of Minnie Hobday and of the police, she had shown the nerve and resourcefulness which he had known would be roused in her by excitement and the presence of an audience. But the morning after a night quite without sleep, alone in the house, she was not to be trusted.

He knew that she ought to go round to the Hobdays' house to inquire after Minnie, but he doubted if he could make her go. She clung to him, needing to be continually reassured that all had gone as he had planned. So when, in the middle of the morning, the police reappeared, Evitt felt from the start at a disadvantage. He felt that he must explain his own presence at home, when surely, of all times, he was needed at the office, and that he must apologise for Rina's failure to be the kind, concerned friend of the bereaved woman.

"My wife's so upset, Superintendent. . . . A bad night . . . Perhaps a prowler around somewhere . . . Afraid . . ."

The words limped out uncertainly. They were bad tactics, Evitt knew, even as he produced them. A murderer should never explain or apologise.

What made it worse was that, for all the notice that Tewson seemed to take, Evitt might not have spoken at all. Tewson had followed him into the sitting-room, had nodded briefly to Rina, who had risen from her chair by the fireplace, then he had stood glancing around the room with the air of looking for something. The fact that he had the air of knowing just what he was looking for made Evitt's plump hands turn to ice.

He crossed to Rina's side. Standing on the grey hearthrug with his shoulder touching hers, he reached automatically for the warmth of the fire. But yesterday's wood fire, for decorative purposes only in this well-heated room, was a heap of ashes.

"I came to tell you," Tewson said, "that Mrs. Hobday has withdrawn the statement she made to us yesterday evening that your clock was wrong. She believes now it was her watch that was wrong. Since it was practically speaking right when she reached home, she suspected you at first of having altered your clock and lied to her about your call to the exchange, in order to create a false alibi for yourself. But now she thinks she must have unthinkingly re-set her watch while she was here."

Tewson had been looking at the grandfather clock while he was speaking, but now his eyes rested on Evitt's face.

Evitt gave a grave nod, almost a bow. He was striving to assume a solemnity of sorrow for his dead friend and partner. It made a slowness of utterance, while he chose his words, seem fairly natural. But he found it difficult to keep his feet still.

"I see," he said. "May I ask what made her change her opinion?"

"Her watch went on gaining after she got home," Tewson said.

"Ah, I see. Just an unfortunate coincidence then."

"Was it?" Tewson gave a tight-lipped, ferocious smile. Then he moved away. He crossed to the telephone and stood looking down at it. "That's what she believes herself. An unfortunate coincidence. But I'm not so sure. . . ." He had picked up a little writing-pad from beside the telephone, the kind of pad intended for the jotting down of messages. From across the room its cover had looked as if it were of tooled leather, of emerald green and gold. But in fact it was of painted metal, cold to the touch of his fingers. "I'm not sure that I agree with her. Mrs. Evitt, what did you do with the pencil that belongs to this pad?"

Rina started. Evitt could feel the trembling begin in the arm that was pressed against his. But her voice was only a very little higher than usual. No one who did not know her well would have noticed it. With an audience to play to, he thought, you could always rely on her.

"The pencil?" she said. "Why, I—I don't know. Isn't it there?"

"I mean the pencil, a green and gold pencil, with which, as Mrs. Hobday told me this morning, you kept tapping her wrist yesterday afternoon, her left wrist, all the time you were playing bridge—tapping her watch too pretty often, of course," Tewson said.

"Did I do that?" Rina asked. "I don't remember. Oh, you don't mean that *that* could have upset her watch!"

Evitt took it up quickly. "No, Superintendent, surely you aren't suggesting that you can deliberately make a watch go wrong—because I take it that that's what this might imply—by giving it gentle little taps with an ordinary pencil."

"No, not an ordinary pencil," Tewson said. "That isn't what I'm suggesting. But I know these pads. The pencils that go with them have magnets in them. That's to make them hold on to the metal covers of the pads, the idea being that you won't mislay them. Neat, if you can be bothered with that sort of thing. And if you keep on tapping a watch with a quite powerful magnet, you can make it go very wrong indeed. You can't tell *how* wrong, of course. You can't tell if it'll go fast or slow or stop altogether. All you can be pretty sure of is that with that magnet drawing at the works, they're going to be badly enough upset to make the watch useless as evidence against a fine old clock like that and a faked call to a telephone exchange. Where *is* that pencil, Mrs. Evitt?"

There was silence in the room. For a moment the Evitts stood close to one another, both tense, wary but wooden-faced. Then Rina drew away from her husband, clawed suddenly at his round, empty face with her nails and started to scream at him.

SAFETY

The strange thing is that when Sidney Sankey taught Roddie Bourne to play with matches, it was done without the least intention of harm, either to the child or to anyone else. If a destructive element in Sankey's nature revealed itself in the ideas he had of playthings suitable for a child of five, he himself was unaware of it. Indeed, the instruction of Roddie in this perilous entertainment was probably as innocent an action as Sankey ever performed, for it occurred during the time of extraordinary happiness for him in his friendship with Roddie and with Roddie's family.

When Sankey first met them, the Bournes, like him, were newcomers to the small Midland town of Bardley. Oliver Bourne, who was thirty-eight, had been in the infantry throughout the war and had been teaching boys for ten years before he arrived in Bardley. He had come as senior history master to the school where Sidney Sankey had just been given the first, and as it turned out, the only job he was ever to have, teaching a little of practically everything to the younger boys.

The friendship, which began as one between Sankey and Bourne, caused surprise in their colleagues, for the two men had almost nothing in common. Bourne was a quiet but ambitious man, brusque and strong-willed, who took a somewhat arrogant pride in his work and his power over his pupils. Sankey was excitable and voluble, but timid, with a fear of the boys whom he had to teach, which was immediately recognised by them and

ferociously exploited. He had become a schoolmaster only because he had been unable to think of anything else that he
might do better, and for this he despised himself and the whole
profession of teaching, and hated the boys. That both he and
Bourne were strangers in Bardley was at first the only thing that
drew them together. Later, however, there was Mary Bourne.
There was also Roddie.

Without Roddie the situation could never have developed.
Mary Bourne was lonely and bored in the unfamiliar town. She
had gone to it reluctantly from a small market-town in Somerset
only for the sake of the extra money, which would help with
Roddie and perhaps make it possible for her to have a second
child. She had taken an instant dislike to Bardley, feeling per-
sonally outraged at the sight of the blackened walls of its build-
ings, of the specks of soot that settled each day on the window-
sills of her home, of its drab little rectangle of garden, of the
squealing trams on which she had to ride whenever she went to
the shops. But she was as fond of her husband as she had ever
been, and had no thought of solving the problem of her boredom by a love-affair with another man. If Sidney Sankey there-
fore had started his visits to her merely for the sake of seeing her
when Oliver Bourne was absent, it is unlikely that she would
ever have allowed them, as she did, to become more and more
frequent. But Sankey always came to see Roddie.

That he arrived to see Roddie surprisingly often when Bourne
was kept late at the school by a committee-meeting, or other
business of which a junior master was free, ought to have
aroused Mary's suspicions. But she was not particularly vain and
not at all perspicacious, and though she was only five years older
than Sankey, there was something about him which made her
think of him as nearer Roddie's age than he was to hers. In spite
of his fear and hatred of adolescent boys, Sankey sincerely
delighted in the company of the very young and had a surpris-

ing talent for amusing them. Often Mary left him to play with Roddie in the sitting-room while she cooked the supper in the kitchen, and Roddie's shouts of pleasure and Sankey's softer laughter, as they played some game that Sankey had just invented, helped to delude Mary that it was only for mothering that he came to her, and to feel the warmth around him of a home, instead of the chill of his lodgings.

She still clung to this delusion even after she had realised that for the first time since she had married him, her husband was seriously jealous.

His jealousy first flared up on the evening when he found Roddie playing with matches. Coming home just after Sankey had left the house, Oliver Bourne found his son kneeling on the hearthrug, near to a blazing fire, with several match-boxes emptied on to the rug before him. He was using the matches to build a little village of log-cabins. For his age, Roddie was deft with his hands and he had been well instructed. The log-cabins were neat, square, well balanced and well roofed and he had every reason to be proud of them. But the matches were not even safety matches, and the sight gave Bourne the excuse that he had been wanting far more than he had realised to lose his temper. Not that any kind of matches would have been any safer so close to the fire, but there seemed to be some added wantonness in having put such things into the hands of a child.

He gave a shout, "Mary—come here!"

She called back, "In a minute."

"Come at once!" Bourne shouted. "Come and see what your child's doing!"

His voice, the sheer rage in it, brought a protesting wail from Roddie. Mary came running from the kitchen. Her face, which was a softly pretty one, with rather plump cheeks and big, mild grey eyes, was flushed from the heat of the cooking-stove, but she grew pale as she took in the scene before her.

Before she could speak, Bourne said furiously, "Didn't you *know* he was doing this?"

Without answering him, Mary dropped on her knees beside Roddie and scooped the matches up into her apron. It was a stupid thing to do, for it made Roddie, who did not in the least understand what he had been doing wrong, start screaming with disappointment and hurt pride. But the sight of the child with all those matches so near to the fire had momentarily filled Mary with blind terror. Besides that, she was not accustomed to Oliver in the kind of rage that he was in.

He was standing rigidly at the edge of the hearthrug, ignoring Roddie, fixing his bright, angry stare on Mary's face. He was a short man, with thick, powerful shoulders, a short, thick neck and a big head, a heavy forehead and a square, heavy chin.

"How long has he been at it?" he demanded. "How long is it since you troubled to find out what he was doing? And where's the fire-guard?"

The fire-guard was where he could see it, in a corner of the room. Supposing that he knew this, Mary answered a question that he had not asked.

"Sidney must have forgotten to put it back," she said. "He was here with Roddie until a minute or two ago. He's only just gone."

"Sidney's good at forgetting a lot of things, but never the time when I'm expected home." Bourne's voice shook with the violence of his feelings. "And while he's here you forget about Roddie."

Aghast, returning her husband's stare with blank bewilderment, Mary's face flushed as swiftly as a moment before it had lost its colour. In all the years of her marriage, it had never occurred to her that Oliver could say such a thing to her.

Seeing this, Bourne's face also reddened, and with a shrug that was halfway to an apology, he went to fetch the fire-guard and place it in front of the fire. But then, because the guard was seldom left there unless Roddie was alone in the room, Bourne removed it again and put it back in the corner, muttering confusedly as he did so, "The man must be crazy, doing a thing like that. Anyway, where did all these matches come from?"

"He must have brought them himself," Mary said. She was still kneeling on the hearthrug, with the matches heaped in her apron, while Roddie stamped and cried before her. "He didn't mean any harm by it."

Bourne by now was beginning to feel hot with embarrassment at the feelings which he had allowed himself to show, and because of this he appeared to accept what Mary had said with a readiness that was far from sincere. The harmlessness of Sidney Sankey was something in which Oliver Bourne never quite believed again. But he was too angry with himself for his self-betrayal to say so.

"Well, that's a change at least," he said, and managed a short laugh. "He usually pockets things. It's become the hardest thing in the world to keep cigarettes in the house since he's taken to coming here. And matches, actually, were becoming practically extinct."

"He's always bringing things for Roddie," Mary said as she stood up and went to the door.

"Mary . . ." Bourne began.

She paused in the doorway.

"Mary, what I said just now . . ."

"I've forgotten it," she said distantly as she went back to the kitchen, where a good piece of steak had had time to spoil and some potatoes to boil to a pulp.

Instead of attending to this now, Mary stood still in the middle of the kitchen, looking down at the matches in her apron. She had not forgotten Oliver's words. In fact, she was only just beginning to feel the full shock of the anger that they had caused in her. As she felt it, she also felt for the first time, in a way that startled her, that Sidney Sankey was intensely important to her.

It was not, she assured herself quickly, that she was in love with him. Wasn't she years older than he was? Wasn't she happily married? And weren't they all nice people, she, Sidney and Oliver?

But still, as she stood there alone in the kitchen, aware from their voices in the sitting-room that Oliver, in his brusque way, was now comforting Roddie, promising him that if it mattered to him so much, he should have matches to play with, only matches that wouldn't be dangerous, there sprang to life in Mary a sense of Sidney as someone whom she could not bear to do without. For a long, bleak moment it seemed to her that if she took heed of Oliver's jealousy, if she stopped Sidney's visits, there would be nothing left for her in this grim town, where she had no other friends, but its blackness and the specks of soot that eternally settled on the window-sills and the hideous trams that went squealing past.

But that she felt this so strongly frightened her, and as soon as she had recognised the feeling, she decided frantically that Sidney's visits must stop.

It was one of the causes of the disaster that was to follow that Mary's mind all too often worked in this way. Just as her panic on seeing Roddie playing with a heap of matches so close to the fire had made her snatch them away from him without giving herself time to think of what this might do to Roddie, so her panic on realising how important to her Sankey's visits had become made her blindly determine to deny herself those visits, without first trying to find out what those visits meant either to Sankey or to her husband.

When, a few days later, she nerved herself to the point of telling Sankey that he must not come to the house so often, indeed should not come at all unless Oliver invited him, she was so bemused by the sense of her own loss that although she noticed the flash of something strange in Sankey's eyes, she did not recognise it as a warning.

She and Sankey were sitting facing each other in the chairs on each side of the fireplace, with Roddie engaged on an ambitious building project with the safety matches that his father had given him on a table well away from the fire. She had begun by telling Sidney of Oliver's anger on finding Roddie playing with matches, then she had spoken less directly of Oliver's jealousy. The cowardice in her nature had made her choose to play her little scene when Roddie was there, for his presence gave her an excuse to speak evasively and the right to expect Sidney to do the same. Laughing at Oliver for being so ridiculous as to be jealous, she asked Sidney if he did not agree with her that however ridiculous one's husband might sometimes be, one ought not, if one cared for him, to let him feel unhappy.

It was then that she saw that strange look in Sidney's eyes. But it was followed at once by one so vague and blank that Mary started to wonder if he was really listening to her. He was often abstracted, given to long silences which sometimes even Roddie found odd, while at other times he was so talkative that no one else could get a word in. The changes on his thin face, with the slightly prominent, dark eyes, the long, sharp nose and the small, lop-sided mouth, matched the changes in his mood. In a mood of animation his expression had a gay, vivid, curiously innocent quality which gave him a kind of good looks, but in one of his withdrawn moods the look that settled on his face was dull, sullen and unattractive.

It was with such a look now and only a slight, unusual mottling of his face, that he continued to gaze at Mary as she went on.

"I think perhaps it's just because he's generally worried and worn out," she said. "I mean, it isn't really like Oliver to act as he did. And that's why I'm more worried than I would be if—well, if he was really that sort of person. I mean, I know he's found this new job a strain, and he's tired and he keeps having headaches. And so I'm really anxious that he shouldn't have the chance to upset himself over anything so silly. You understand?"

She hardly knew that she was being dishonest. But Sankey knew it. He was exceedingly sensitive to the feelings of others, even if his interpretation of what he perceived was often distorted. He knew that Mary was concerned, not for her husband's peace of mind, but for her own. She was thinking only of herself, not of Oliver, and of course not of Sidney Sankey.

As he still did not answer, Mary said nervously, "Sidney, you do agree with me, don't you? You do understand?"

"Oh yes, I understand," he answered absently, staring straight through Mary at some dim images that had begun to form at the edges of his mind. "I'm usually fairly understanding."

"Oh, you are," Mary said. "That's why I knew that I could talk to you about it all."

"But I'll miss you—and Roddie. At first."

Sankey looked at Roddie and frowned slightly. They looked so alike, Roddie and his mother, with their round, softly moulded faces, grey eyes and soft, fair hair, that it had felt natural to love them both with the same love, as if they were still part of one another. Playing with Roddie, feeling happy at the warmth of the child's response to him, Sankey had felt as if this response were Mary's too, as if it were merely by some accident that the arm that had slid round his neck was Roddie's and not hers, that the eager breath on his cheek was the little boy's and not the woman's.

A mistake, of course. A very foolish mistake.

Standing up and crossing the room, Sankey put out a finger

and gave a sharp jab at Roddie's latest and largest log-cabin. The matches toppled over in a heap.

Mary gave a little cry. "Oh, why did you do that?"

"Why do we do any of the things we do?" Sankey asked indifferently as he turned away to the door.

Mary did not follow him to see him out, for as she looked at the heap of matches on the table and at Roddie's bewildered face above them, suddenly, for the first time, she was frightened of something that was in Sidney Sankey and not merely in herself.

She tried to shake off this fear, yet it stayed with her throughout the evening. Oliver Bourne, coming in presently, saw that something was wrong. But he also saw that a packet of cigarettes that he had left on the mantelpiece had disappeared. This meant that Sankey had been there, and because of the rage that always overcame him now whenever he thought of Sankey, Bourne did not trust himself to ask Mary what had happened.

Sankey that evening walked all the way back to his lodgings instead of taking the tram. A thin mist of rain was falling. In the light of the street-lamps the pavements had a slimy sheen. The air felt like a sodden blanket wrapped around him, clinging to his thin body with a chill that started him fiercely shivering. He turned up the collar of his coat, sank his head between his shoulders, buried his hands in his pockets, but did not think of walking faster. With his gaze sliding along unseeingly over the muddily gleaming paving-stones and oily puddles, he strolled along, chewing his lower lip and sometimes suddenly whistling a half-bar of music.

But when he reached his lodgings he was jolted out of his abstraction by the discovery that he had no matches in his pocket with which to light the gas fire in his room. He had only a packet of cigarettes which he did not remember having bought. Like many very heavy smokers, he had never been able to come to terms with a petrol lighter, for apart from the fact that he was one of the people in whose hands any gadget immediately goes wrong, he had found that a lighter never had enough fuel in it to last him long. Yet only a few days ago he had bought half a dozen boxes of matches, so where were they now? Of course, at the Bournes' house. So he would have to go downstairs and ask his landlady to help him out.

At the thought he flung himself down on the bed in the cold room, clutching his head and pouring out frantic, childish curses, of a kind that he thought he had forgotten until this moment of shattering pain.

During the next few weeks Sankey thought a great deal about Mary Bourne, not with love or tenderness, but with a deep, revengeful concentration. When he met Oliver Bourne in the school, the two men scarcely spoke to one another. But Sankey was very much on Bourne's mind. Though he had never discussed the matter with Mary, he knew that the scene that he had made had driven her to tell Sankey to stay away from the house. That she had done this had been a great relief to Bourne, yet whenever he passed Sankey in the corridors of the school building, or saw him in the staff commonroom, saw the unhealthy blotching of his sullen face and the way that his dark eyes evaded his own, an uneasy conviction developed in Bourne's mind that he and Mary were not at the end of their troubles with Sidney Sankey.

Among the other masters it was generally said that Sankey would never last the year out. He was too inefficient, too helpless with the boys, too lazy. But the year, what was left of it, often seemed to Bourne a long time, too long to be endured without taking action of some sort. Only he did not know what kind of action to take. And really there seemed to be nothing that he could do about Sankey but, like the other masters, leave him alone.

To have left him alone, to have continued leaving him alone, would have been far the best and safest course for the Bournes to pursue, the best and safest for themselves and the best and safest for Sankey. He was almost intolerably unhappy at the school, was suffering badly from sleeplessness and eating so little that even his indifferent landlady had begun to worry about him, but the image of Mary was fading from his mind.

He had almost managed to blot out of his memory the sweetness of the evenings that he had spent playing with Roddie while Mary went ahead with her cooking, calling out to them occasionally from the kitchen, her voice intimate and gay. If he gave a thought to the few occasions when he had been quite alone with her, it was no longer to think of her as gentle and desirable, but as really rather insipid. At the same time, when now and then he tried his hardest to make his first clear anger against her, that confident, humiliated hatred, blaze up as fiercely as at first, the flames required a tiresome amount of stoking. So if Mary had not happened to meet him in the town one Saturday afternoon and to invite him to go home with her for tea, there need have been no tragedy.

Mary gave him the invitation because her own feelings about him had completely changed. She was far happier than she had been during those first weeks in Bardley, because now she had plenty of friends. There was the wife of one of the other schoolmasters, who had a little boy of Roddie's age and whom Mary saw nearly every day. There were her next-door neighbours, a middle-aged couple who had begun an acquaintanceship cautiously by commenting on the weather over the garden wall, but with whom Mary and Oliver now spent frequent evenings, eating large quantities of homemade cake and being instructed in local politics. There were the members of a choral society to whom Mary had been introduced. In this altered situation, Mary knew that she had no reason to fear the strength of her own feelings for Sidney Sankey, and on catching sight of him, looking idly into a shop-window, as usual, alone, she thought only that she had really been extraordinarily unkind to him and that it would be pleasant, would be a load off her conscience, to make it up to him by asking him to tea.

She did not notice that he started to tremble when she spoke to him, and the hoarseness of his voice when he answered her only made her think that perhaps he had a cold and hope that he would not pass it on to Roddie.

His answer was a confused excuse for not having tea with her, yet he started to walk along beside her, and Mary had no doubt that he was pleased and grateful. His failure to give any answer at all to what she said next, and the way that he avoided looking at her, did not seem to her particularly strange. Hadn't he always gone in for these trance-like silences? She talked for both of them, apologising cheerfully because it was so long since they had seen one another, and because she had nothing special at home for tea, and because Roddie, when they arrived at her home, showed so little interest in his old friend.

"It isn't that he's forgotten you, it's just that he's shy," she said. "He's always talked about you a lot, and he keeps making us play those games you taught him."

Roddie looked up at his mother with a little frown. Of course he had not forgotten Sidney, but he was not shy either and he did not understand why she should say that he was, when usually she complained that he was too eager to thrust himself forward. If he wasn't bothering much to talk to Sidney now it was simply because, as she knew, he had a friend of his own age and so could get on very well without the help of a grown-up who stayed away for weeks at a time without any explanation.

Sidney, glancing down, sensitive as always to the moods of others, saw all this in the child's face, and his mouth, normally a little crooked, dragged further still to one side. He hardly knew what was happening to him. He seemed to be split in two, one part of him feeling a deadly fury against both mother and child, the other part feeling all the old, comforting sweetness in their presence.

Mary, going to the kitchen, made tea and hot buttered toast and opened a packet of biscuits, and bringing the tray into the sitting-room, found Sankey looking thoughtfully at a drawing-board that was balanced on a stool, on which Roddie had recently constructed an elaborate, cathedral-like structure out of safety matches. A little patronisingly, Roddie was explaining to Sankey how he had supported the walls and the spire with fuse-wire and pins. Sankey, nodding, had a curiously dazed look, as if he could not follow what the child was saying.

The one part of him had suddenly thought that all that he had to do now was absently to put a cigarette in his mouth, light it and drop the still burning match on to Roddie's cathedral. Almost as if he had already done it, Sankey could see the whole building burst into one great flame. Then he had only to knock over the drawing-board so that Roddie's clothes caught fire. Mary's work-basket happened to be on the floor nearby, with a heap of what looked like net for curtains, which she was hemming, spilling out of it. The stuff would flare up at a touch. And Roddie would scream, Mary would come running to him, would try to beat out the flames, her own clothes would catch fire and her hair, her soft, fair hair . . .

"He did it all by himself, you know." Mary had put down the tray and had come to Sankey's side. "Neither of us helped him at all. The fuse-wire was all his own idea. We feel a little proud of him."

She was standing so close to Sankey that her sleeve was brushing his. Her hair, with the lamp-light shining on it, curled on her forehead and against her smooth, plump cheeks. To touch, it would feel like silk. It had a faint scent that seemed to him intimately and uniquely Mary's.

Sankey gave a deep sigh, pocketed the packet of cigarettes and the box of matches that he had just absent-mindedly taken from the mantelpiece, reached out clumsily and drew Mary to him. He was aware that her body stiffened against his and that she made an attempt to draw away from him, and then that she stood quite still, but he was not aware how fiercely his arms were crushing her. He had again started trembling violently and had tears in his eyes. Nothing in the world seemed to matter except that he should bury his face in her hair and forget the image of the flames.

But Oliver Bourne, coming in at that moment from the study where he had been correcting homework, felt his reason consumed in a roaring flame of hatred. Somehow he had the presence of mind to grab Roddie, thrust him out of the room and close the door before picking up the heavy brass poker from the fireplace and bringing it down on Sidney Sankey's skull.

As Mary shrieked, Bourne struck again and again. It was only as Sankey's limp body slumped to the ground that the madness died out of Bourne's face, leaving it as dull and empty as Mary had sometimes seen Sankey's.

As she stumbled away from them both to the door, Bourne let the poker slip out of his fingers on to the carpet.

"Wait!" he croaked.

Mary turned, leaning against the door, clutching at it to stop herself falling. She had thought at first, when she saw her husband with the poker held high over Sankey's head, that he meant to kill her too, and her fear of him had not begun to lessen.

Bourne muttered something that seemed to be mainly a repetition of her name, then again he said hoarsely, "Wait!" Pressing his hands to his temples, he stood quite still, looking blankly at

Sankey's body, as if he knew neither what it was nor how it had come there.

Mary could not bear to look at Sankey. She kept her eyes on her husband's grey, vacant face and so saw expression return to it. For a moment this seemed as terrifying as the sight of Sankey's battered head, for the expression that appeared, business-like, determined, competent, was one so familiar to her, so normal, that it left her straying wits no possibility of escape from the knowledge that this man whom she knew so well, was a murderer and had always had it in his nature to commit this murder.

Bourne stooped and searched quickly through Sankey's pockets. All that he appeared to be searching for were his own cigarettes, for as soon as he found them he straightened up, thrusting them into his own pocket.

"Mary, can you handle Roddie?" he asked sharply.

"Handle him?" she said helplessly.

"Persuade him that he didn't see Sankey today."

"I don't know how."

"Then persuade him that he must never tell anyone about it. That it's a secret."

That seemed to her less impossible, since Roddie loved secrets.

"I can try," she said.

"Then go on—do it."

"What are you going to do—with—?"

"I'll tell you when I've done it. For now, just remember you never saw Sankey today. You or Roddie. You haven't seen him for weeks."

"For weeks," Mary echoed stupidly, then she turned swiftly, jerked at the door-handle and escaped from the room.

As soon as she was out of it she started to cry hopelessly and noisily. The sound brought Roddie running to her. She cried fairly often, yet whenever she did so he always had the feeling

that it was something unbearable that had never happened before, and that he would do anything in the whole world to stop
it.

Today what he had to do, it seemed, was to promise never to
tell anybody that Sidney Sankey had been to the house. Well,
that was easy. He wasn't interested in Sidney any more and
didn't see why anyone else should be. But the trouble was that
even when Roddie had given the promise, his mother's tears did
not stop, for Mary had a terrified conviction that she had forgotten something that was vital to Oliver's safety, and what was
almost worse than that, had a wild horror of even trying to remember it.

The news of Sidney Sankey's death was in the newspapers
the next day. His body had been found, late in the evening, on a
railway line a short distance from the town. In the short para-
graph devoted to this fact, no mention was made of foul play
being suspected, and Sankey's landlady was quoted as having
said that she really wasn't at all surprised, because, poor boy, he'd
been in a terrible state of depression for a long time. Next day
that was what Sankey's colleagues said too, both among themselves and to a detective inspector who appeared at the school to
ask a few not particularly searching questions.

All of the masters to whom he spoke, and that included
Oliver Bourne, said that they had all noticed and been greatly
worried by Sankey's recent air of dejection. Some of them said
that they had wished that they had known how to help him,
others remembered prophesying that he would not last the year
out. The detective inspector went away, looking not specially interested or thoughtful.

But that was because he had trained himself not to show interest or thoughtfulness, except when it might be useful to do
so. In fact, something that had happened while he had been

talking to the senior history master had roused his interest and struck him as deserving more than a little thought.

During that interview Oliver Bourne had been smoking a pipe. It had gone out, and to re-light it, he had brought a match-box out of his pocket, taken out a match and tried to strike it on the match-box. But the match had failed to light. Cursing absently, Bourne had thrown the match into the wastepaper-basket and accepted a light from the inspector. This had happened more than once.

The last time that it occurred, just as the inspector had been leaving, Bourne had not troubled to return the match-box to his pocket, but had left it lying on his desk, and the inspector had unobtrusively pocketed it himself. On his way back to the police-station he verified what he thought he had observed about the matches while talking to Bourne. They were safety matches, yet the box that they were in was of the kind intended for matches that will strike on anything, from the sole of a boot to a thumbnail. And that, the inspector thought, was an odd thing to carry in your pocket, since it was entirely useless.

The uselessness of it, the complete pointlessness of having carefully filled an ordinary match-box with safety matches, made it a far odder thing to carry than the safety match-box filled with ordinary matches which the man found dead on the railway line had had in his pocket. The inspector, as a matter of fact, had not thought that there was anything particularly unusual about those matches in that match-box. He had supposed that Sidney Sankey had run out of the safety matches that he had probably been in the habit of carrying, and had been helped out by someone who had happened to have only the other kind. Even now the inspector did not attach overmuch importance to the complementary character of the match-boxes in the two men's pockets. However, several people had told him that the Bournes were the only people in Bardley with whom Sankey had even tried to make friends, so in spite of Bourne's statement that he had scarcely spoken to Sankey for a couple of months, the inspector decided to pay the Bournes' home a visit.

He was not, until he reached it, looking for a murderer, but only for the motive for a suicide. Yet as soon as he had entered the Bournes' sitting-room, he started to ask himself certain questions. Why, for instance, did a patch of the carpet look as if it had been recently washed? Why was the heavy brass poker on the hearth so bright that it could only have been cleaned that morning, when the other fire-irons and the brass fender had the faint tarnish which in the atmosphere of Bardley clouded metal surfaces after a day or two? Why were Mary Bourne's eyelids swollen with weeping and her eyes blank with fear?

Oliver Bourne had not yet come home from the school. When the inspector, accompanied by a self-effacing sergeant, rang the doorbell, Mary had been sitting by the fire, mending one of Roddie's jerseys, while Roddie had been playing in a corner, adding a wing to his cathedral. He took no notice of the inspector's arrival, or of the things that he and Mary said to one another about Sidney Sankey, for when Roddie set to work, designing, building, creating, he was wholly absorbed. Even when his mother and the stranger started talking about him he did not pay much attention, because, of course, as people always did, they just talked about how dangerous it was for a little boy like him to be playing with matches, and that was pretty boring.

"Yes, we were worried to death when he started it," Mary said, "and we tried to get him interested in bricks and Meccano and everything else we could think of. And I suppose that was our mistake. The more we tried to keep matches away from him, the more set he was on matches and nothing but matches. You know how children are. And they were difficult to keep away from a boy who's as active as he is. He'd find them wherever we hid them. So we gave in and got him to promise he'd only play with the ones we gave him and only in the corner over there, away from the fire."

"And he keeps his promises?" the inspector asked.

"Oh yes," Mary said. "A promise . . ." But that reminded her of the promise that Roddie had given her the day before and of what would happen if he broke it, and her voice dried up. She had to clear her throat before she could go on. "A promise is a very serious thing to a little boy."

"And you give him safety matches," the inspector said, "in the non-safety sort of box, so that he can't possibly light them."

Mary was surprised at how quickly he had guessed Oliver's device for protecting Roddie from the dangerous consequences of his passion.

"Yes, and my husband uses up the non-safety matches on his pipe, keeping them in the safety match-boxes we've emptied," she said, "and we leave them up there on the mantelpiece and Roddie never touches them because of his—his promise." On that word her voice dried up again. She raised a hand that felt icy cold to her mouth.

She knew now what it was that she had forgotten the evening before when she had seen Oliver searching through Sidney's pockets to recover the packet of cigarettes which he had guessed would inevitably have found their way there and which would certainly have Oliver's fingerprints on it. She had forgotten the box of matches, which she had actually seen Sidney pocket at the same time as the cigarettes, as she came into the room with the tea-tray. She had forgotten them because she had not wanted to remember. With the unconscious craft of her new fear of her husband, she had kept her secret to herself until she knew that the police also knew it.

That they did know it was clear, for there were the two match-boxes, or two just like them, side by side in the inspector's hand.

Oliver Bourne, coming in at that moment, saw them also, understood how he had blundered in his absent-mindedness, helping himself to one of Roddie's boxes, and thought, as he had thought the day before, that he had again caught Mary in an act of betrayal. His rage was as sudden and violent as it had been the day before, yet it was still against Sidney Sankey and all that he had done to the Bournes, beginning with his crazy instruction of a child of five in the pleasure of playing with matches. It was at the image of Sidney Sankey that Oliver hurled his lighted cigarette, though where it fell was on Roddie's cathedral.

It was as if Sankey's dream of revenge, the dream that he had discarded in horror, had after all come true.

The cathedral roared into a sheet of flame. Mary screamed and snatched at Roddie. As she swung him away, one of his shoes caught a corner of the drawing-board on which the cathedral stood and overturned it on to the new net curtains that she had been hemming.

But it was not Roddie's clothes, or Mary's, that the flames leapt to consume. It was at Oliver, who was standing nearest, that they sprang, at the same moment as the quiet sergeant wrenched at the hearthrug and hurled it at the burning mass in an attempt to smother the flames.

He might have saved Bourne if Bourne had let him. But he only fought him off, trying madly to escape both from the man and the fire. And in a sense Bourne did escape from the police, for he died that night of shock and burns in the hospital.

A VERY SMALL THING

Nobody saw the letter until they moved the dead old man. His head had covered it as he lay sprawled across the desk, and while the photographers had taken their photographs and the fingerprint men had done their work, the envelope had remained hidden. But when at last the ambulance men had lifted the body on to the stretcher to take it out of the room, there was the letter, lying on the blood-stained blotter, stamped and addressed.

A letter, of course, was to have been expected. It had been the absence of one that had given Detective Superintendent Mellor the itchy feeling that this was not the simple suicide that it had appeared at first glance. Suicides nearly always leave letters. And the dead man's housekeeper, who had found the body after she had got home from a visit to her sister and had telephoned the police, had told them tearfully that Mr. Crick was the kindest of men, the most considerate. But it was not the act of a kind and considerate man to end his life without leaving behind the letter that said that no one but himself was to blame for his death.

However, there was the letter on the desk, so perhaps it was suicide after all.

The envelope was slightly splashed with blood and the writing on it was shaky, but it was perfectly legible and it was addressed to Detective Superintendent Mellor.

That took him by surprise.

He had the envelope fingerprinted before he opened it and

was told that there were only smudged prints on it, except for one on the stamp, and that the probability was that they had all been made by the dead man. It was the same with the single sheet of paper that Mellor found in the envelope.

The letter was brief.

"Sir, This is to confess to you that I am the murderer of Miss Christine Beddowes, of The Beeches, Grove Avenue. I will not go into my motive for killing her, except to say that I had thought that we were to be married, but apparently I was mistaken. Now I find that I cannot live with what I have done and am about to take my own life. I am, Yours, etc., A. Crick."

Mellor showed the letter to Sergeant Arkell, who was standing beside him.

Arkell remarked, "Very formal. Signs it as if he was writing to the newspapers."

"He was a solicitor," Mellor said. "Perhaps that made him formal about murder. A. Crick—I wonder what the A stood for."

"Arthur, sir." The housekeeper, a wrinkled little woman who appeared, now that the body was gone from the room, to have lost the fear that she had had at first of coming into it, looked expectantly at Mellor, as if she hoped to be allowed to read the letter too.

He did not show it to her.

"Do you know a Miss Christine Beddowes?" he asked.

"Miss Beddowes who lives next door? Yes, of course I do," she said.

"Did Mr. Crick know her well?"

"I don't know what you mean by well," she said. "He was a neighbourly sort of man, always said good morning and that kind of thing, but she wasn't his sort."

"In what way not his sort?"

She shrugged her shoulders in a way that expressed a certain disapproval of Miss Christine Beddowes.

Mellor put the letter back into its envelope.

"Well, it's time we went next door," he said to Arkell. "I suppose that's where we'll find her. There's no point in trying to conceal a body if you're going to kill yourself too straight after the murder—though it's true the letter sounds as if he didn't know he'd feel like suicide till after he'd done the job."

"Murder?" the housekeeper cried. "Who's talking about murder? Who murdered who?"

"That remains to be seen," Mellor said. "But I'm afraid we're going to find Miss Beddowes next door with a bullet through her brain. I hope to God he made a neat job of it. If there's a thing I hate, it's a messy shooting."

Mellor strode out of the room and Arkell followed him.

They went next door to The Beeches, a spacious bungalow which was almost hidden from the street by a high beech hedge. But Mellor, as it turned out, had been only partly correct about what they would find there. He had been right in thinking that Miss Beddowes would be at home, but when she opened the door to them, it was evident that she had no bullet in her brain, or anywhere else in her well-proportioned body. She was a slender woman of about twenty-eight, with bright greenish eyes touched up with a good deal of eye-shadow, heavy, straight hair of a not very convincing shade of auburn, that fell to her shoulders, and she was wearing a pale green housecoat of some thick, luxurious-looking silk.

Mellor identified himself and the sergeant and asked if they might come in.

"Of course," Miss Beddowes said. "I'm glad you came. I saw the police cars and the ambulance next door, and I knew something awful must have happened, and I thought of coming over to ask if I could help, but then I thought I'd only be in the way, and that if you wanted me you'd come here." She led them into a big, bright sitting-room furnished with what Mellor thought were some very oddly shaped chairs and low tables, and with some strange sculptures standing about that consisted mainly of holes. "Has something happened to poor Mr. Crick?"

"He's dead," Mellor said. "Shot, sitting at his desk. His house-keeper found him."

"Shot? D'you mean he shot himself? He committed suicide?" Her voice went high and shrill. Her voice was the least attractive thing about her. It was high and nasal. "But why? Why ever should he do a thing like that?"

"His letter said it was a suicide," Mellor replied. "But it also said he'd murdered you, which happens not to be true. So perhaps the rest of it isn't true either. What do you think about that, Miss Beddowes? We thought perhaps you could help us to sort it out. First, had you ever been engaged to him? His letter implied that you had. Had you broken it off recently?"

She sank down into one of the deep armchairs, the skirt of her housecoat flowing out around her.

"I don't understand it," she said. "He wrote that he'd murdered me? Whatever could he have been thinking about? And we were never engaged—certainly not. Well, that's to say . . ." Her fingers plucked at the silk of her skirt. There was rather more tension in her face than Mellor had noticed at first. "Perhaps it's just possible he misunderstood our friendship. It never occurred to me before, but he was an old-fashioned sort of man, you know. He may have taken me more seriously than I realised. How sad—how terribly sad. Because his mind must have gone at the end, mustn't it, if he believed he'd murdered me? And he was such an intelligent man."

"When did you see him last?" Mellor asked.

"Two or three days ago," she said. "At the weekend. Yes, it was on Sunday. He came in for a drink before lunch, as he often did."

"Did you quarrel?"

"Oh no. No, it was all just as usual. I think we talked mainly about our gardens. We generally did. We hadn't much else in common. He didn't stay for long."

"How long have you known him, Miss Beddowes?"

"About a year. He called on me with a basket of vegetables from his garden soon after I moved in. He was always very kind. He was a widower, you know, and I think he was lonely."

"But on Sunday he seemed to you quite normal? Not depressed, not excitable, not overwrought?"

She gave a shake of her head. But then she frowned.

"As a matter of fact, I did wonder if he wasn't feeling well. He was more silent than usual. But I didn't give it much thought. He was a quiet sort of man."

"You see, he did a rather strange thing this evening," Mellor said. "Apart, I mean, from confessing to a murder that he hadn't got around to committing. He put a stamp on the letter he left on his desk, addressed to me. I find that distinctly strange."

"A stamp?" she said. "Is there anything strange about putting a stamp on a letter?"

"Who was going to post that letter?" he asked. "Not Mr. Crick himself. And when his housekeeper found him, as he must have known she would, she called the police in the natural way, by telephone."

Miss Beddowes gave a bewildered shake of her head. "I don't understand. I can only think that if he was in the state of mind to think that he'd murdered me, he didn't know what he was doing."

"Of course, that's possible," Mellor agreed.

"A stamp's a very small thing," she said.

"Very small. All the same, I'd like to know how you spent the evening, Miss Beddowes. Say from about eight o'clock to ten."

She stiffened in her deep chair. "How *I* spent it? What are you thinking of?"

"I'm thinking," Mellor said, "that Mr. Crick, having a legal sort of mind and wanting to leave everything in proper order, might have written his letter to me earlier in the evening, intending to come here, kill you, then on his way home post his letter—there's a letter-box just outside, I noticed—then go home and kill himself. But something prevented him doing what he intended. Somebody could have known just what he was going to do and got into his house and shot him before he himself could commit murder."

"Someone?" She pressed a finger against her breast, pointing at herself. "Me? You're thinking of me?"

"I only asked you how you spent the evening," he answered.

She gave a soft laugh and seemed to relax. "Then I'll tell you. I went to a party given by Mr. and Mrs. Wheeler, who live at number twelve Grove Avenue. I got there about eight o'clock and I came home only a little while before you got here. I'd just had time to change out of my evening dress when you arrived."

"Will Mr. and Mrs. Wheeler be able to say that you didn't disappear even for a little while during the evening?" he asked. "Number twelve can't be very far from here."

"Oh yes, they'll be quite sure," she said. "So will several other people. It was quite a small party. If I'd vanished for a time it would certainly have been noticed. I'm not a murderess, Mr. Mellor."

"Then I can think of only one other explanation," Mellor said, "and perhaps you can help me with it. For instance, I'm sure you can tell me whether the man who did the murder is still here, or has he gone away without you? You were just going to leave with him, weren't you, when we showed up? You're fully dressed under that handsome housecoat."

Catching Arkell's eye, he gave a slight nod and Arkell went quietly out of the room.

"I may as well tell you," Mellor went on, "that if he hasn't gone already, it's too late now, because the house is surrounded."

As he spoke there was the sound of a shot in the garden. It was followed by excited cries, then by a voice shouting orders.

The woman leapt to her feet.

"The fool, I told him it wouldn't work!" she cried. "But he said after the old man saw him he'd got to get rid of him, and he said I'd got to go with him, because he was sure, if I didn't, I'd talk. Oh, the fool! As if I'd ever have talked. But he never trusted anybody."

"And no doubt he said he'd manage it so no one would wonder why you'd disappeared," Mellor said. "We were supposed to be looking for a dead woman, not a live one."

The door was thrown open and Arkell reappeared, accompanied by a constable. Between them they had a man who was struggling fiercely as each of them gripped him by an arm. He was a short, squat man with crudely shaped features, which, in spite of their coarseness, bore a faint resemblance to the delicate features of the woman.

"Nobody hurt," Arkell said. "He tried shooting it out, but Fred here got him."

"Ah, I see, I see—one of the old familiar faces," Mellor said. "Your brother, Miss Beddowes? Though his name was Hewitt when I heard of him last. How long since you escaped from Parkhurst, Hewitt? Three days? Seems it was hardly worth the effort. And Arthur Crick saw you here this evening, getting ready to leave, and recognised you, didn't he? He'd seen you in court some time, I suppose. But how did you persuade him to write that letter before you killed him? By the threat of a beating-up, was it? He knew you were going to kill him anyhow, but in return for that letter you did it painlessly. But as your sister said, he was a very intelligent man. With you standing over him, he quietly put a stamp on the envelope. I expect that seemed to you a quite normal thing for him to do. But in fact he was leaving me a message that that letter wasn't what it seemed. So even if the two of you had got away in time, we'd have tracked you down sooner or later. Now you can both come along to the police station."

And wearily, because he had had a long day and knew that there was a long night ahead of him, Mellor added the words of the official warning.

SCATTER HIS ASHES

On nights like tonight, about the beginning of December, I often suffer from an attack of depression and insomnia and find myself wandering about the house, feeling that there is something special that I ought to be doing, but not knowing what it is. I find myself wanting a cigarette, although normally I am a non-smoker. I start wanting to ring up friends on the telephone for no particular reason.

My husband understands these moods of mine and does not interfere with me. He is a very kind and tolerant man. He knows that the moods generally come on about the anniversary of the night my father died. That is how I like to put it to myself. I think, I speak, of the night he died, or passed on, or passed away, and my husband does the same. But both of us know, of course, that what we are doing is only avoiding saying, "the night he was killed, the night he was murdered." Time does not soften the brutality of those words. If anything, it makes them crueller. After twenty years I find I shrink from using them even more than I did at the time, when there was no evading them.

Tonight my mood is an especially bad one, which is why I have started to write down some of my feelings. I should like to be rid of the past, and perhaps writing of it may help. I have heard people say that it does, and at least it is something that I have never tried before. I have tried travel, drink, even drugs. But the ghosts always return and while they are with me they utterly destroy the orderly contentment of my life, which I value beyond everything.

I know that the weather tonight is half the trouble. All day long it has looked as if it were going to snow, yet no snow has fallen. That is how it was on that day twenty years ago. About halfway through the morning the daylight grew murky and as I went about my usual work in the house, I started turning on lights in all the rooms. My father shouted at me from his downstairs bedroom that this was another example of my recent, insane extravagance, but really I could not see without the lights. Thick clouds had spread quickly over the sky. It was dark grey and looked like a dirty old pillow, ready to burst and spread its white feathers all over the city.

Feathers . . .

There I go, thinking of them again.

I had a dream about them last night. I dreamt that I had bought a new fur coat. As it happens, I already have four, my new ocelot that my husband gave me for my birthday, and my old mink, which was one of the first things I bought for myself when I inherited my money, and a very smart, short black sealskin jacket, which is about two years old now, and the musquash, which my father let me buy I do not know how many years ago and which I still keep for running around the shops. But last night, in my dream, I bought a fifth coat. I do not know what I thought the fur was, but it was dark grey and soft and silky. And then, when I got it home, I found that the coat was not made of fur at all, but all of feathers. Nothing but feathers. For some reason, this was terrifying. The dream turned into a nightmare and I woke up, shivering with panic.

My father had been sleeping in that downstairs room for several years before his death. He had bad arthritis, a bad heart, some trouble with his kidneys, and had had a slight stroke. Our doctor once said to me jovially that Mr. Greenbank had at least six illnesses which ought to have killed him, but that he would probably outlive us all. I almost believed this. I saw him as indestructible. Half helpless as he was, he clung to life with a kind of ferocity, growing murderously angry with anything that struck him as a threat to his security.

I think, in his situation, I should have been glad to die, but his limited, crippled life was astoundingly dear to him.

He was sure, from the start, that my marriage threatened him. I told him, I swore to him, that I would never leave him as long as he needed me, that Garry was going to move into the house with us and that that would mean that my father would have more help than before, not less. He only muttered some of the ugly words that he liked to use and asked me jeeringly if I really did not know that Garry was only marrying me for the money that would one day be mine, and was he likely, that being so, to trouble himself much about my poor old father?

Perhaps I should explain here that my father could not stop the money coming to me. I am sure he would have, if he could. But it had been my mother's, most of it willed to my father only for his life-time, and when he died it would be mine. I sometimes think that that will of my mother's may have been one of the reasons why he had that bitter determination to live on and on. For when he died he would lose all his power over me, except through what he had managed to make of me while he was alive, and that was the only power he had left over anyone. He had once been managing director of a big firm that manufactured woollen goods, and had had a lot of power over a great many people, but now his world had shrunk to me and the few old cronies who still came to see him sometimes.

I was thirty-two when I married Garry. My mother had died when I was fifteen, so my father had had seventeen years in which to mould my character. Garry was three years younger than I was. He was a small man, which for some reason I found intensely attractive. I am big myself, tall and lumpy, rather like my father, with an indifferent complexion and thin, mouse-brown hair. The sort of good-natured charm that I am told I possess now had had no chance to develop then, because I was about as lacking in self-confidence as a young woman can be.

Garry's hair was fair and curly and his eyes were a vivid blue. All his movements were quick, vigorous and decisive. He had immense vitality. And he had a number of habits which I thought of as wholly, uniquely masculine and so accepted as somehow peculiarly endearing. He was extremely untidy. If he opened a drawer to take something out, he never thought of shutting it again, but assumed that someone would always be there to do it for him. When a shirt, or socks, or his underwear were soiled, he simply dropped them on the floor, knowing that I would pick them up and put them in the linen-basket. He was a chain-smoker, and used only to aim his cigarettes in the vaguest way in the direction of an ashtray. But he never said anything wounding or spiteful. He was generous with presents. And as for him having married me for my money, he had a good job with a big firm of estate agents in our northern town, and soon after moving into our house, he took to paying the house-keeping bills himself, to save me the humiliation, so he told me, of having to ask my father for the money. Also, Garry paid for our wedding reception, when, of course, my father should have done it.

My father would not come to the wedding and would not have the reception in our house.

"I don't want a lot of people here whom I don't know from Adam," he said, "eating and drinking and making a racket. It wouldn't be good for me. If you want to do such a damnfool thing, go on and do it, I can't stop you. But count me out of it."

So we had the reception in an hotel, and there, for the first time, I met Garry's brother, Alec.

If there was one thing from the first that I did not like about Garry, it was Alec. I know that sounds absurd. A man's brother is not a part of him. Yet, as it happens, Garry and Alec were more a part of one another than brothers usually are. Both their parents had died when they were boys, leaving them very badly off, and Alec, who was five years older than Garry, had always looked after him until he was able to stand on his own feet. So I did my best to see the good in Alec. It must be there, I thought, if Garry could be so fond of him. He was in the habit of consulting Alec about everything. He used to quote the things Alec said, kept telephoning him, and from time to time, if some specially difficult problem connected with his work came up, went up to London to stay with him overnight. For Alec was in the London headquarters of the same firm as Garry and had helped him to get his job with them.

But Alec was a noisy, vulgar man, red-faced, thick-necked, burly, with sly little eyes under thick lids with hardly any eyelashes, and he thought it was funny to be rude and ask such things as whether I couldn't find a wife for him just like myself, rich and beautiful. He was drunk by the time he said it, and I could see how embarrassed Garry was, because even he never made out that I was a beauty. So I pretended to be amused and said that I would do my best, at which Alec flung an arm round me, gave me a great kiss on my cheek and said, "Ah, there aren't any more like you, love!"

Garry and I had no honeymoon, as my father could not be left alone for long enough for us to go away. Mrs. Clarke, our daily, who did not mind coming to sit with him in the evenings when I went to the Townswomen's Guild or to a concert, could not possibly have looked after him for a whole weekend. So as soon as the reception was over, Garry and I went back to the house and began our life together there. Garry went to the office on Monday morning and I went on doing the cooking, as I always had, as well as a fair amount of the housework. Mrs. Clarke, who came for three hours each morning, was too old, and the house was too big and inconvenient, for her to be able to manage it by herself. Garry asked me once if I would not like someone younger to work for me, or even a maid to live in, but I knew what an upheaval like that would do to my father, after the shock of my marriage, so I said I was perfectly happy with things as they were.

In fact, I was unbelievably happy. I had never minded doing the cooking and the housework. I had never been trained for anything else. And I went out so seldom that if I had not had some kind of work to do, I should long ago have died of boredom. And now I had Garry to cook for and look after, and for the first time in my life had the glorious experience of hearing my cooking praised when I had taken the trouble to make something specially good, and of being thanked for doing little things for him, so little that sometimes I was hardly aware that I had done them.

What a lot Garry taught me about living! I discovered my own body through him. There I was, thirty-two, and I had never known what a body was meant for. It was like being given the gift of life for a second time. I also learnt how much two people can enjoy themselves just talking together over a bottle of good sherry in the evenings, telling each other things which I had never dreamt it was possible to share with a single soul. You had no need of other friends if you could do that. There was also the joy of being told, not that I was incompetent, lazy and indifferent to the sufferings of others, but too kind for my own good, sweet-natured, gentle and in need of cherishing.

And always there was the delight of simply seeing Garry about the house, small, taut, vital, male. I loved simply to sit and look at him and think of nothing but him.

The flaws in my happiness were Alec and the silent war between Garry and my father. It became a silent war, not an open one, very quickly, when my father discovered that Garry never answered back. To sarcasm, unkind innuendoes and violent tirades, his only answer was a rather odd smile, as if he were enjoying a joke that could not be shared with anyone, not even with me. Then he would go out of the room and quietly do whatever he had meant to do all along. So Garry was always easily the victor and my father learnt to avoid quarrels which he was sure to lose.

Garry tried to teach me the trick of it. He said, "A man on crutches or in a wheelchair can't follow you all over the house, so when he annoys you, why don't you simply leave the room?"

"But he doesn't often exactly *annoy* me," I said. "It's much more complicated than that."

"I know," Garry said. "He frightens, bullies, hypnotizes you, so you think you have to stay there and take it. But you haven't really, you know. He hasn't any power over you. It's you who have power over him. You can leave him any time you choose, and at the back of his mind he knows it."

"But he's very fond of me in his own way, don't you see?" I said. "I couldn't hurt him."

"I wonder if he is fond of you," Garry said, "or ever has been of anyone. I can't see him caring for anyone but himself."

"Oh, he adored my mother," I said. "He simply worshipped her."

"That's what he says now," Garry said. "But I wonder what she'd have told you herself, if you'd been old enough to ask her."

This was such a shocking thought to me that I was silent. My whole relationship with my father had been built on the assumption that he had loved my mother with all his heart and that it had been his hideous suffering on her early death that had warped what had once been a fine and generous nature. For she must once have found him worth loving, after all, and my memory of her was of someone who had a lot of rich affection to give and cheerfulness and charm.

"Have you ever thought," Garry went on, "that he may have married her for her money and that that's why he's so certain I married you for yours?"

I looked at him stupidly. I have always had a slow mind and it takes me time to assimilate a new idea.

He gave his easy-going laugh.

"You don't think I don't know that's what he thinks about me, do you?" he said. "He came straight out with it the very first time we met. He doesn't bother with subtleties."

"Well, anyway," I said after a moment, "I could never leave him. It wouldn't be right. I told you that before we married."

"Good lord, I wasn't talking about *leaving* him," Garry said. "Not leaving the house, moving away. I understand how you feel about that and it's quite all right with me. No, I just meant, when he says something that gets under your skin and makes you go dead white—do you know you do that?—just get up and walk out of the room. Leave him to stew in his own juice for a little. That's all I meant."

"Oh, I see," I said, relieved, because I dreaded an argument with him.

"Only you'll never do it," Garry said with a smile, and reached out and punched my cheek lightly with his fist. "You're too damned easily put upon. You just ask to be trodden on. Well, don't ever let me do it. If you ever find me treading on you, my darling, yell."

The funny thing was that I wanted to yell, though of course I never did, at his devotion to Alec, at his clinging to him even now that he was married, at his dependence on him or whatever it was. Actually I was never quite sure which brother was the more dependent on the other. It must have begun by the older brother supporting the younger, but by now Garry was so much the more intelligent and wide-awake of the two that I thought perhaps this had been reversed. In any case, I hated the relationship between them. Even if Alec had been a person for whom I could have felt some affection, I should have hated it. I wanted Garry all to myself.

I used always to feel nervous and restless during the long telephone conversations that he and Alec used to have with one another. There was nothing private about these conversations. The telephone was in the sitting-room and Garry used to sit comfortably on the sofa with his feet up and the telephone to his ear, smoking cigarette after cigarette and spraying ash on the carpet and chatting on and on to Alec. Sometimes it was about something that had happened in the office, some mistake that Garry had made and was worrying about, or something that a client had said. Sometimes it was about nothing in particular. And as I listened, a weird sort of feeling that was almost like hatred used to well up in me, hatred not of Alec, which would have been silly but understandable, but of Garry himself. I used to get stiff and cramped in my chair with the effort of fighting the violence of the feeling. It frightened me a good deal.

But I felt even worse when Garry went to London to see Alec. On those occasions Garry never stayed away for more than one night and he always telephoned me in the evening from Alec's flat and had a long conversation with me, of much the same kind as he had with Alec. But every time that he went away I became possessed by an utterly irrational, feverish anxiety that I would never see him again. I used not to show it. I would kiss him good-bye quite calmly, tell him in an unemotional, automatic way to drive carefully, and go back into the house and shut the door before the car was even out of sight. But then I would go frantic.

I would not sit down and cry, though I always felt as if I should like to. I would start to rush about the house, doing all sorts of unnecessary jobs, turning out drawers, moving pieces of furniture, and as likely as not, breaking something. I would polish, scrub, clean windows, re-arrange books, and cook enough to last the household for at least the next three days. I would keep this up until the evening, when Garry's telephone call came through.

Usually this was at about ten o'clock. If it was much later than that I would go up to my room, because my father became fractious if he could hear me moving about downstairs when he wanted to go to sleep, and I would take the call on the extension up there. At last then I would be at peace. I would take my sleeping-pill and sleep soundly. I did not normally take sleeping-pills, but on those nights when Garry was away and my mind became obsessed, you might say almost unhinged, with terrifying premonitions of disaster, I used to take three grains of sodium amytal and have a quiet night.

At this distance, it all seems so ridiculous. I cannot think of anything that would make me act like that now.

My fears of disaster did not take any specific form. They were like a child's fear of the dark, in which the special terror is that the perils thronging it are unimaginable. I did not see, oh no, my God, I did not see even a shadow of what was actually to happen!

It began one day in early December, when Garry set off on one of his visits to Alec in London. It was bitterly cold. The sky was the colour it has been all day today, that dirty grey that threatens snow, and it seemed to have sunk down so low that it almost rested on the roofs of the houses. There was black ice on the garden path.

It was after lunch that Garry set off for London. It was a six hour drive. I warned him that the roads would be treacherous and as usual I begged him to drive carefully. He patted my shoulder, kissed me and told me not to worry. He was a good driver, wasn't he? he asked me. I agreed that he was. I did not, as a matter of fact, worry much about his having a crash on the road. I did not imagine the car going into a skid, shooting over the edge of a bank, turning over and over and bursting into flames, or else perhaps going head-on at seventy into a lorry. I was not afraid of anything so rational. As he got into the car I turned back into the house and quietly shut the door behind me.

Soon I began to wish that the snow would come, although I knew that it would be unpleasant for him to drive through, because there was a curious tension in waiting for it. It gave me the feeling that time had stopped and that the day and the solitary night ahead of me would never come to an end. But by the time that full darkness came and I went round the house, drawing the curtains, no snow had fallen yet. There was no wind either, but only a silent, lifeless chill that seeped into our big, old-fashioned rooms through the chinks round the badly fitting sash windows and the great blank panes of glass.

My father and I had steak and kidney pudding for dinner, followed by apple charlotte and custard and biscuits and cheese. Afterwards my father hobbled into the sitting-room on his crutches to watch television for a while before going to bed, and when I had done the washing-up, I joined him. But the programme he was watching was not one that I cared about, and my usual devil of restlessness entered into me and I returned to the kitchen.

I made a chocolate cake of which Garry was particularly fond. I made a trifle with plenty of brandy in it. I made a chicken casserole with mushrooms, which I thought we could have for dinner the next evening. I made a plum tart, using some plums that I had bottled in the summer. I made an apricot flan. By then the kitchen was wonderfully warm from the heat of the oven and full of good smells, but it was ten minutes to ten and Garry had not rung up yet.

I leafed through one of my cookery books, looking for something new to try. Then all of a sudden I decided that I had had enough of cooking and would vacuum the sitting-room carpet instead and give the furniture an extra good polishing. I knew my father would have gone to bed by then and the room would be empty.

I did the polishing first. There is something to be said for that heavy old mahogany. It does show results when you polish it. I quite enjoyed doing it. Then I got out the vacuum-cleaner and went to work on the carpet. I had all but finished when I realised that the door had opened and that my father, in his dressing-gown and leaning on his crutches, was in the doorway.

There was a puzzled sort of fury on his face. He said something to me that I did not hear because of the buzz of the vacuum-cleaner. I switched it off and in the silence the sound of his voice burst on me like a shout.

"You're mad!" he roared at me. "Do you know that? That man's driven you out of your mind. You were always weak in the head, but now you're actually insane. What time do you think it is?"

"I'm sorry," I said. "I'm afraid I wasn't thinking. It's just that I get restless when Garry goes away. I never get used to it."

"You were used to it for long enough before you got married, weren't you?" my father said. "You didn't seem to mind being alone in those days. You didn't start using that damned machine in the middle of the night."

"It isn't actually the middle of the night," I said. "It's only a little after half past ten. I didn't think you'd want to go to sleep yet."

"Who said I wanted to go to sleep?" he demanded. "I want to read and I want to read in peace. I can't do it with that devil's racket going on."

"But you always read the paper while Mrs. Clarke uses the vacuum in the mornings," I said.

He answered, "Of course I do. I know she's got to use it. I know the house has to be kept clean and you can't get a woman to go down on her knees nowadays and do a job of work like her mother did. I know all that. I'm not unreasonable. But there's a time for everything. At half past ten at night I expect quiet. I've a right to quiet—even if I haven't many other rights left in this house."

"I'm sorry . . ." It occurred to me that half the things I said to my father used to begin with those words.

"Oh, you're sorry." His big, sallow face began to crumple as if he were about to cry. It sometimes did that in his attacks of self-pity, though tears never actually came. "D'you know what, you aren't sorry at all. You've no heart. You do things like that on purpose, just to goad me, just to try to make me get angry. You know it isn't good for me to get angry. You know about my heart. You know about my arteries. You know anything could happen to me any time if I ever lost control of my feelings. And you say you're sorry!"

It was at times like this that I went silent. Something seemed to lock up everything inside me. I'm sure my face turned white, as Garry had told me it used to. I stood there, holding the handle of the vacuum-cleaner, thinking of all the things I might have done if I had been a different kind of woman. For, big as he was, my father was really very helpless. He was a great, half-lifeless, ruined hulk of a man. He was at my mercy. He had been for years. But I just stood there, silent.

He began to turn away, moving clumsily on his crutches. But then he paused and looked straight into my face with his puzzled, fierce eyes.

"You'll never understand," he said. "You haven't the brains to understand, and I'm no good at putting things. But I've always tried to do what was best for you. I've thought of you before anything else. I promised your dear mother I would, and I have, I swear to God I have. I tried as hard as I could to save you from getting into the clutches of that cheap little crook you married, and I'm trying still. I'm trying to go on living, though I'm pretty sick and tired of it, let me tell you, to stop him getting his hands on your money. Because you'll give it all to him, every penny you've got, you're so simple-minded. And as soon as you do, you'll have seen the last of him. That'll be the end for you. That'll be the end of your fine daydream. But tell you that— what's the use?"

I came to my senses then. It was the attack on Garry that did it. I remembered what he had told me to do. Quietly I wound up the cord of the vacuum-cleaner, wheeled it past my father out of the room, put it away in the cupboard under the stairs, and went up to my room.

My father called something after me, but I did not listen. I closed the door behind me, threw myself down on the bed and found that I was shaking all over. But inside I was joyful. I had won. I had been all by myself, scared, but I had won. Garry was right, I could always win. When I heard my father's crutches thumping slowly across the hall downstairs as he returned to his room, I had to jam some of the eiderdown into my mouth to stop myself laughing aloud.

An eiderdown is full of feathers . . .

When I think of it I can still feel the rasp of the rose-coloured satin against my lips. The feathers seem to be choking me. I want to be sick.

It was nearly eleven o'clock and I was in bed reading when the telephone rang. I picked it up and the operator said, "Mr. Willis is calling you from London and wishes you to pay for the call. Will you accept the charge?"

Garry always did that when he rang me from Alec's flat, so that the cost would go on our bill and not on Alec's.

I said impatiently, "Yes, please go ahead."

There was the usual click, then Garry's voice said, "Darling? I'm sorry it's so late, but Alec insisted on taking me out to dinner and a theatre he'd got tickets for and we've only just got in. How are things?"

"Fine," I said. "Wonderful."

"Now, what's all this?" he said. "Things aren't supposed to be wonderful when I'm away. You're supposed to worry all the time. Or haven't I understood you in the past?"

"Ah, of course you have," I said. "I've been on edge all day, just as usual. But what I meant was, my father came and talked to me all about you, and I simply walked out. He said horrible things about you, and I simply walked out."

"Now, that really *is* fine," Garry said. "I'll make an adult woman of you yet. What were the horrible things he said about me? Just the usual?"

"Oh, don't let's talk about them," I answered. "None of it matters. I'm beginning to grasp that things that simply aren't true don't matter. You can laugh at them. Tell me about the play."

"It's not worth talking about either. It was just a lot of nonsense about people popping in and out of bed with the wrong people, and losing their trousers and falling over the furniture. I found it hard work to raise a laugh, even to please Alec, but he seemed to enjoy it. Then he wanted to drop into a pub on the way home, so I couldn't help being late, could I?"

"It doesn't matter," I said.

"I thought perhaps I shouldn't call you at all," he said. "I thought perhaps you'd have taken your sleeping-pill already and gone to sleep."

"I never take it till after you've rung," I answered. "If you hadn't, I'd just have lain here awake, waiting."

"Well, take it now and have a good night."

"Yes, I will. And you take care, driving home tomorrow, won't you?"

"Of course. I always do. Good night, darling. I love you."

"Oh Garry . . ." My voice broke and I could not get out what I wanted to say. There was too much love in me for me to be able to direct a trickle of it into something so small as the mouthpiece of a telephone. I held it tightly for a moment, then gave a deep sigh and put it down. Reaching out for the capsule that I had put ready on the bedside table with a glass of water, I swallowed the pill, turned off the light, lay back on my pillows and slept deeply and dreamlessly.

The alarm clock woke me at seven o'clock. I always got up then to make my father his morning tea. Then I would have a bath, get dressed and cook the breakfast. It was still dark. It was still very cold too. Going to the window, I expected to see the pale glitter of snow in the darkness, but everything was utterly black. I did not like it. There was something eerie and threatening about that icy barrenness. I put on my dressing-gown and slippers, went downstairs, made the tea and carried it into my father's room.

I know I am very slow in my reactions. Some people take this for stupidity. Cleverer people realise that I am simply very slow. I need time to put together what I see, what I think and what I feel. I need time to understand. But in the end I do. Indeed, I do.

What I saw as I stood there in the doorway was whiteness. It was all over the bed and the carpet and the furniture. Also I saw a great jagged hole in the plate glass of the window, through which a freezing draught was blowing in. It was as if the draught had blown a snowstorm into the room, although there was no snow outside in the garden. The whiteness stirred gently here and there in the current of air from the window.

Of course, it was not snow. It was feathers. Someone had pressed a pillow down over my father's face and the pillow had burst and the draught had carried the blizzard of little downy feathers all over the room. But the pillow had done its work. My father was dead.

Because I am so slow, I stood there for some seconds before, quite gently, I let the tea-tray slide out of my hands and fall with a crash. Hot tea splashed over my feet and bare ankles. I began to scream. Naturally, there was no one to hear me. After a moment I stopped. I did not go near the bed, for I knew my father was dead and that there was nothing I could do for him. There was a feather on his face, just by one of his nostrils, and it was motionless.

Turning, holding to the wall as I went, because I was so dizzy, I went to the sitting-room, dropped on to the sofa and picked up the telephone.

I was going to dial 999.

But just before I started, I noticed a disconcerting thing. It caught my attention, made me wonder, frown, then thoughtfully put the telephone down again.

On the carpet, close to where I was sitting, was a little heap of cigarette ash.

It was on just about the spot where Garry had a habit of letting his ash fall during those long conversations that he used to have with Alec. But I had been over that part of the carpet the evening before with the vacuum-cleaner. I knew I had. I remembered moving the sofa so that I could clean the spot where it usually stood, as well as all round it. Moving that heavy old sofa was a thing that you remembered.

But now there was a little heap of ash where there could not be one.

My first impulse was to put my slipper down on it and flatten it into the carpet and forget about it. For ever. But then my mind began to work. Thoughts began to come to me. Slow, slow thoughts.

At first only one was clear. Garry had been here last night.

It was not easy to believe, but it was easier than to look at that heap of ash and convince myself that I had missed it with the vacuum-cleaner, or simply that it did not exist. I had to face it, he had been here, had sat just where I was sitting and had smoked a cigarette.

Drawing my feet up under me on the sofa, I clasped my arms tightly round me to keep out the awful chill of the room. But the chill was in my own blood, seeping out of my bones. I started shivering and found that I could not stop it.

I started thinking of all sorts of unimportant things, like the chocolate cake that I had made, and a pink feather hat that I had bought a few weeks before that Garry had said he liked, and some gold cuff-links that I had seen in a shop a day or so ago which I had thought of buying for him, but had not, because I was too unsure of his tastes. I often wanted to buy things for him and then did not, because I never trusted myself to guess what he would like. I had had very little experience of buying presents for anyone and was so nervous of choosing the wrong things, which he would only thank me for out of politeness, that possibly I had appeared ungenerous. That was a wretched thought. I brooded on it for a while as I sat there and shivered.

Then, with a jolt, I thought again that Garry had sat here in this room. He had smoked a cigarette. He had talked to me on the telephone.

But how can you ring up a person on an extension of the telephone you are using yourself?

I began to think that I would like a cup of tea. I went out to the kitchen, where the kettle that I had used to make the tea for

my father was still warm, and made another pot and took it back
to the sitting-room and sat down on the sofa again.

By then I understood how the telephone call had reached me.
It had been Alec who had telephoned from London and asked
the operator for that transferred charge call. Then, as soon as it
had rung here and I had picked up the telephone by my bed,
Garry had picked up this one. And so we had been connected
and had been able to talk to one another. He must have been sitting here quietly, waiting for the call to come through, for some
time, and smoking as usual and forgetting to notice where his
ash fell. All as usual. It was such a familiar scene, I could see
him doing it. How could he know that the last thing that I
would do before going to bed would be to vacuum the carpet?

The trouble about thinking is that you cannot always stop
when you want to. I shut my eyes and pressed my knuckles
against them.

I thought, "My father was right all along. Garry and Alec,
they had it all planned from the beginning. A convenient marriage to a lonely, unwanted woman who would be rich when her
sick old father died. A simple murder. And now . . . I wonder
what they've got planned for me."

I opened my eyes again and gazed at the little heap of cigarette ash.

It was so small that the first policeman who came into the
room might easily put his foot on it and tread it into the carpet.

Hesitantly my hand went out to the silver cigarette box near
the telephone. I took out a cigarette, put it between my lips and
lit it. It made me cough and the smoke got into my eyes and
brought tears to them. I had smoked only one cigarette before in
my whole life. That was when I was sixteen and had wanted not
to be left out among the other schoolgirls. But I had not liked it
and had never smoked again. I did not like it now. But I smoked
that cigarette from beginning to end, adding to the little heap of

ash on the carpet and scattering the rest of the ash carelessly about, some on the sofa, some actually in an ashtray, and finally taking the stub to the lavatory and flushing it down the drain, in case it had fingerprints, or traces of my saliva, or something like that on it, which would show that it had not been Garry who had smoked it.

Then I dialled 999.

I told the police, when they questioned me later, about having vacuumed the carpet in the evening, but I never said anything about the ash. But of course they saw it and worked out for themselves what it meant, and once their suspicions were aroused, it did not take them long to break down Garry's alibi. They explained it all to me after they had proved that he had not been in the theatre with Alec, and that neither of them had been in the public house where Garry had said that they had gone for a drink, and that someone had seen him in a café on the road to London, where he had been stupid enough to stop for a snack in the early morning. He had not in fact been in London at all the day before. He had actually stayed hidden in our garage, where he had known that I had no reason to go, as he had the car. Then when he had seen the light in our bedroom go on and had known that I had gone to bed at last, he had let himself quietly into the house and gone into the sitting-room to wait for Alec's call. It had been made specially late on purpose so that he and Alec could be sure that I should be waiting for it in bed and not downstairs. And after Garry had talked to me, he had gone to my father's room and smothered him.

Smothering can sometimes be mistaken for a natural death, particularly with someone as old and ill as my father. Of course it had been intended to look like a natural death. But the pillow had burst and the feathers had floated all over the room, so there had been no hope of disguising the fact that it was murder. So then Garry had smashed the window, to make it look like a case of breaking and entering, and had taken my father's wallet and his gold watch and chain. But he had thrown them over some hedge on the way to London, where he had gone straight after the murder, and where, by the time I discovered it, he had been in bed, asleep.

In those days they still had hanging.

It was not long before I was a widow and a rich widow too. I sold the house and moved away, and I reassumed the name of Greenbank, though I stuck to the title of Mrs. I had some bad times at first, because I had no friends or outside interests, and sometimes I used to drink too much by myself and take too many barbiturates. Then one day I bought myself that mink coat I mentioned.

It was a gesture of liberation. After it I began to find it easier to spend money on myself and to start doing things that I had only had dreams of before. It was about a year after my father's death that I went to a travel agent and made arrangements to take a trip round the world. I bought a lot of new clothes for it, all totally different from anything that I had ever worn before, and I had my hair cut short and tinted. I was feeling like an exciting stranger to myself when I set off, with my mind full of all the new sights that I was going to see, and the new people that I should meet, and the friends I should make.

What actually happened is that before we had even reached Madeira I met the man who later became my second husband. We were drawn to each other from the start, and spent a great deal of time in each other's company throughout the voyage. There was no question of falling in love. I suppose there never has been. But we have a great deal of affection for one another, we trust each other and enjoy being together. He is twenty years older than I am, has more money than I have and suffers from rather poor health, which makes him require a good deal of looking after. But with my experience, that is not too much of an effort. He was a widower when we met, whose first wife, whom he had worshipped, had recently died. So in some ways, I suppose, you could say I am almost back to where I started.

The difference is that my husband, compared with my father, is a kind and considerate man, who makes me feel that he likes me and values what I do for him. I consider myself, on the whole, a very lucky woman. We have spent almost eighteen years together. It is only occasionally, on a day like today, about this time of year, that I feel all sorts of disturbing emotions stirring inside me, and a kind of wildness threatens to do strange things to my brain.

The real tragedy, of course, is that it was all so unnecessary. If Garry had ever loved me, as he pretended he did, if he had relied on me instead of on Alec, if he had trusted me, he need never have tried to deceive me. We could have worked together. Among my daydreams there had often been one of getting rid of my father and being finally free to be myself, and with Garry's initiative and forcefulness behind me, I might really have done something about it. And I should never have blundered as he did. I am a more capable woman than people realise. At least, if I had used a pillow, it would not have been one that would burst, spilling those horrible feathers everywhere. The death would really have looked like a natural death. Or natural enough to deceive that silly old doctor of ours, who thought that my father ought to be dead anyway of six different diseases. There would have been no difficulty about a death certificate. Everything would have gone smoothly and we could have been so happy. . . .

But Garry never loved me. That is the thought that I have to concentrate on when my mind starts to run on in this way and a sort of grinding pain starts up in my heart. Everything he said to me, everything we did together, was founded on lies. All our happiness was only something he let me imagine for a little. My father was right about him from the start. Garry himself proved it to me. He showed me up to myself as everything my father had always said I was. I suppose that was why I had to destroy him.

UNDUE INFLUENCE

"Why, Evelyn!" Mrs. Gosse exclaimed. "What a lovely surprise! I never dared to expect you."

"And how very, very naughty of you not to have let us know what happened straight away," Evelyn Hassall said, stooping to kiss the old wrinkled forehead, sallow against the snowy white of the pillows. "To leave it to that daily of yours to tell us—which it took her a fortnight to think of doing. We only had her letter this morning."

"Ah, Mrs. Jimson, so well-meaning, but she shouldn't have bothered you." Mrs. Gosse smiled up at her niece as she stood by the bedside, holding a bunch of jonquils and some magazines. "But it's sweet of you to have come. I know what a busy life you lead."

"Well, really! The hospital people should have phoned me at once."

Mrs. Gosse was touched by the concern in Evelyn's voice. Yet the truth was that the old woman was a little surprised by it. It was two years since Evelyn had been over to see her, and as Evelyn and Oliver lived only fifty miles away, a distance which, if they happened to feel, say, like dropping in for lunch some Sunday, was nothing nowadays, Mrs. Gosse had slipped into the habit of believing that her niece and her husband did not really want to be bothered too much about her.

That occasion, two years ago, when Evelyn, as now, had come over bearing gifts, had been Mrs. Gosse's eightieth birthday party, a lovely party. Her stepdaughter Judith, with her two little girls, had been there, and of course darling Andrew had still been alive then. He had had his coronary about six months later, though he had been a year younger than his wife and no one had ever dreamt that he would die before her. Evelyn and Oliver had not been able to come to the funeral, because they had been away on a Caribbean cruise, but they had sent a beautiful wreath. The strong scent of the jonquils that Evelyn now laid on the bedside locker, saying that she supposed a nurse would bring a vase for them if she rang, made Mrs. Gosse suddenly remember that wreath. And that made her think of death. Naturally she had been thinking of death a good deal since her accident, and sometimes it had been with a dreamy sort of fascination, but more often it had been with a quietly stubborn resistance. She did not want to die yet.

Evelyn sat down on the chair by the bed and undid the collar of her fur coat. She was a pretty woman in a pallid, fluffy-haired way, not much over forty, though she looked rather more, because behind the pink and white softness of her face there was a certain hardness of the bone, a tightness of the muscles.

"Now, tell me what really happened," she said. "Mrs. Jimson isn't the most literate of letter-writers."

"Well, dear, really nothing much happened," Mrs. Gosse replied. "I fell, that was all. I was on the way to the kitchen to get my breakfast, and you know those three steps in the passage —I just tripped there and fell. And I don't really remember much about it, because apparently I fainted—and d'you know, I've never, I really mean never, fainted in my life before. Then when I came to, I was here. So I hardly know anything about it. But I've been told Mrs. Jimson came in at her usual time and found me and got Dr. Bryant at once, and he got an ambulance and sent me here. And it turned out that what I've got is a fractured femur and I'm going to be stuck here for quite a time. But really I'm very lucky, because I understand that a good many people of my age would simply have got pneumonia and died. And they're so kind to me here—nuns, you know, mostly Irish— I've never been called 'darlin'' so often in my life before!"

"Well, it just shows I've always been right, doesn't it?" Evelyn said. "You shouldn't be living alone. I hope Oliver and I can persuade you to be more reasonable about that now."

Actually Mrs. Gosse could not remember when Evelyn had protested at her living alone. Judith, Andrew's daughter, had tried hard after Andrew's death to persuade her stepmother to go to live with her and her husband, Ronald. But Ronald, who was in the oil business, had just been posted to Venezuela, and Mrs. Gosse had not been able to see herself, at eighty, pulling up all her roots and going to live in such a strange and distant place. Besides, loving as Judith and Ronald had always been to her and dearly as she loved their children, Mrs. Gosse had always had a dread of becoming a liability to others, particularly to those for whom she cared the most.

"Anyway, when they let you out, of course you'll come to us," Evelyn went on. "No, don't argue about it. You couldn't possibly go home. You must come and stay with us for as long as you need to."

"That's very kind of you, dear," Mrs. Gosse said. "It's a very tempting suggestion. I suppose I'll find it rather difficult to manage on my own for a time. I'll think it over."

But really there was nothing to think over. It was obvious that even when Mrs. Gosse could move about her ward with her two aluminium crutches and go to the bathroom by herself, she could not possibly have looked after herself in her own flat, with only Mrs. Jimson coming in to help her in the mornings. It was inevitable that she should accept Evelyn's invitation. So when at last Mrs. Gosse left the hospital, it was in an ambulance that was to carry her to the Hassalls' home.

Mrs. Gosse was rather dismayed by the ambulance. She had imagined that she was well enough to make the journey by car. But Evelyn reminded her that her spare bedroom was on the first floor and that as Mrs. Gosse would not be able to manage the stairs, she would have to be carried up them on a stretcher. Regretfully, Mrs. Gosse thought of her own flat, in which she would quite soon have been able to hobble out into the garden to look at the crocuses coming out under the beech trees and to sit on the bench there in any early spring sunshine that might brighten an occasional day, and to pick big yellow bunches of forsythia for the vases in the sitting-room. In the Hassalls' house she would be cooped up in one room until she could go up and down the stairs, and who knew how many weeks that would be? However, it was a very attractive room with pale grey walls and a dark red carpet and pearly white cupboards and some nice photographs of Greece on the walls and a beautiful little bathroom opening out of it.

Oliver carried Mrs. Gosse's luggage up for her. He was a short, rotund man of fifty, a stockbroker, with plump jowls and a bald head, sparsely fringed with dark hair. His eyes were dark, rather protuberant, and looked oddly intense in the pink placidity of his face.

"You see, there's a lovely view from here," he said, waving at the window. "Nothing between you and the downs. You'll enjoy that, won't you? We thought of that when we asked you to come."

"How kind you both are, how very kind to me," Mrs. Gosse said, and just then would have been immensely pleased if she had been able to think of something more to say to make up to the Hassalls for the fact that in the past somehow she had never thought of them as particularly kind people. But no doubt there would be opportunities later to show her gratitude. She only added that she was feeling rather tired and would like to go to bed.

"And you're longing for a cup of tea, aren't you?" Oliver said, and hurried out so that Evelyn could help Mrs. Gosse to undress and get into the bed in which the electric blanket had thoughtfully been turned on, waiting for her.

The next three weeks were very pleasant. It was true that Mrs. Gosse found them rather quiet. She missed the bustle of the nurses round her and the visits of her bridge-playing circle and of faithful Mrs. Jimson. Evelyn sat with her aunt when she could and Oliver generally paid her a visit when he got home from the City, but Evelyn lived a busy life, filled with voluntary work and committee meetings, and Oliver was usually tired in the evenings. And unfortunately the one thing that the Hassalls' spare bedroom lacked was a telephone. Mrs. Gosse loved chatting with her friends on the telephone, and now that she was too far away from them for them to be able to drop in to see her, she would have liked to be able to ring them up and settle down for a nice long comfortable gossip. Always, of course, finding out from the exchange how much the call had cost and paying the sum to Evelyn, for Mrs. Gosse would no more have thought of telephoning at the Hassalls' expense than of allowing them to pay for the stamps on the numerous letters that she wrote to her friends and which Evelyn took to the post for her.

It was the fact that none of these letters was answered that was the first thing that began to worry Mrs. Gosse. She could not understand it. Her friends were not neglectful people. Always, when she or any of them had gone away on a holiday, they had sent one another picture postcards. At Christmas, even when they were meeting every few days, they sent each other greetings. And those who, because of their infirmities or domestic problems of one sort or another, had not been able to visit her in the hospital, had written to her. But now there was silence. It seemed odd. She began to get querulous about it and one day actually asked Evelyn if she was sure that she had remembered to post the letters.

Evelyn laughed and said, "Of course, darling. I don't forget things."

"But I haven't had any answers," Mrs. Gosse said. "I don't understand it."

"You're too impatient," Evelyn said. "Very few people answer letters by return. I know I never do."

"But you're quite, quite sure you did post my letters, are you?"

"Quite, quite sure."

Mrs. Gosse accepted it. Yet a nagging worry remained. She began to feel cut off from the world in a way that slightly scared her. But that, of course, was absurd. There was nothing for her to be afraid of. It was just that her relative helplessness and the long hours that she sometimes had to spend quite alone were beginning to get on her nerves.

Then one day she and Oliver had a rather curious conversation.

It was Mrs. Gosse herself who thoughtlessly began it. Oliver had come into her room to bring her coffee after a particularly delicious dinner that Evelyn had cooked. She was an excellent cook and she understood how much it meant to an invalid to have a meal served on a tray with shining silver and a pretty tray-cloth. That evening there had even been a few snowdrops in a little glass jug on the tray. Mrs. Gosse was touched by the thoughtfulness of it.

"You're really so good to me, both of you," she said to Oliver. "You'll see, I shan't forget it."

Rather to her surprise, he answered with a self-conscious laugh. She had an odd feeling that she had just said something for which he had been waiting. But he said, "Now, now, we don't want to talk about that sort of thing, do we?"

"But I mean it," she said. "You do so much for me and I couldn't bear it if you didn't understand how grateful I am."

"But there's no need to talk about things like that yet, is there?" he said. "Why, goodness me, I expect you'll outlive us all."

"Outlive . . . ?"

Mrs. Gosse was startled. She realised that he had thought, when she spoke of showing him and Evelyn that she would not forget their kindness, that she had been speaking of what she would leave them in her will. But in fact she had simply been thinking of making a present to Evelyn of a pearl and ruby brooch, inherited by Mrs. Gosse from her grandmother, a very charming thing and probably quite valuable, and which she was sure Evelyn would like. And Mrs. Gosse meant to think of something for Oliver too. He was an incessant smoker and there was that gold cigarette-case of Andrew's. Perhaps Oliver would like that.

But she did not want to embarrass Oliver by letting him know how he had misunderstood her.

"Oh well," she said, "we all come to it sooner or later. There's no point in being afraid of thinking about it, is there?"

"Well, of course, I've always hoped that you'd remember Evelyn," he said. "But as the money was all Uncle Andrew's, it wouldn't be surprising if you felt you had to leave your share of it to Judith."

He was watching her as he spoke with disconcerting intentness.

Mrs. Gosse sipped her coffee.

"No, perhaps it wouldn't," she said. "Of course, I made my will thirty years ago and I've never thought of changing it. I remember when Andrew and I went along to our solicitor to-

gether and made our wills at the same time. Not that I'd anything of my own to leave then. It was just to save trouble later if
he should predecease me, as of course happened. We both
agreed about the terms. They were very simple. Dearest Andrew, I would never think of doing anything that I thought he
wouldn't like."

"No, no, of course not, of course not," Oliver said, and his
eyes seemed to fill with a hungry kind of curiosity, as if he were
trying to determine whether the ambiguity of her reply was the
result of deliberate evasiveness or merely of aged muddle-mind-
edness. Then suddenly he went hurriedly out of the room and
let the door shut behind him with a loudness that was almost a
slam.

Mrs. Gosse put her coffee-cup down quickly on the bedside
table because her hands had just started to tremble violently and
she was afraid of slopping coffee on to the flower-patterned
sheets. Clasping them together, she lay there rigid in the comfortable bed, trying to think clearly and not let confusion and a
perhaps irrational panic overwhelm her.

She told herself that Oliver had never had much tact or
refinement and that it was just like him, if he was curious about
her will, to blurt it out as crudely as he had. And what more natural for him than to be curious? Yet there was a callousness in it,
an indifference to her feelings, which offended Mrs. Gosse
deeply. For the question of what would happen to her modest
fortune when she died could be of no interest to Oliver and
Evelyn unless they had already talked freely to one another
about her death. And she was only eighty-two. Her mother had
lived to ninety-three and her father to ninety-seven, and he had
enjoyed a game of bowls on the very day of his death. And as
longevity was said to run in families, surely it was a little impatient, to say the least, of Oliver and Evelyn to be wondering
about her will.

Unless . . .

Unless they had been told something in the hospital about her health that had been kept from her. Was her heart, for instance, not as strong as she believed? Was there anything the matter with her arteries? Had they some reason for expecting her to die soon? And was that why they were looking after her so assiduously, and while they were at it, keeping her virtually a prisoner, denying her all other human contact, perhaps never posting the letters that she had written, giving her no access to a telephone, and now beginning, when she was all too conscious of her complete dependence on them, to suggest to her that she should make a will in their favour?

No, that was all nonsense. She was letting her nerves get on top of her, allowing herself to be overcome by senile suspiciousness. Of course she was not a prisoner. She was being devotedly looked after. She ought to feel nothing but gratitude. All the same, she must think, she decided. She must think very clearly, without getting lost amongst hysterical thoughts and fancies.

Lying still, except that her fingers plucked at the edge of the flowered sheet, she gazed at the ceiling and presently began to make what she thought was really a rather clever little plan. She meant it as something just to set her own mind at rest, and it would be so easy, so simple even for her to carry out that it seemed very sensible to try it. She would do it tomorrow. Having decided on that, she dropped off almost at once into a pleasant doze, from which she did not waken until Evelyn came into the room to settle her for the night and to give her her sleeping-pills.

Mrs. Gosse put her plan into execution next day as soon as she heard Evelyn leave the house to do some shopping. Oliver, of course, had gone off to London some time before. So while Evelyn was out Mrs. Gosse had the house to herself. Moving carefully and slowly, leaning on her crutches, she crossed her room to the door, opened it, went out into the passage and hobbled along it to the door of Oliver's and Evelyn's bedroom. For there was a telephone extension in there. She had overheard both of them talking on it. She had never suggested using it herself because this had never been offered and she regarded bedrooms as private places into which one did not intrude without an invitation. Yet really, with no one to see her, what was to stop her going in and ringing up, say, good Mr. Deane, her solicitor, and asking him to visit her?

She put a hand on the handle of the bedroom door. It did not open. It was locked. The Hassalls did not intend to let her reach that telephone extension to call Mr. Deane or anybody in the outer world. So her fears had not been crazy. She was in fact being held a prisoner.

With her heart beating in a way that frightened her, she made her way back to her room.

At the head of the stairs she stood still and looked down. There was the front door. There was escape. If she gritted her teeth at the pain, could she somehow get down the stairs and reach the street?

But what would she do when she got there? Wave her crutches at passing cars? Hope that the driver of one of them would not think she was mad and would give her a lift of fifty miles to her home?

Probably before a car stopped Evelyn would be back and gently forcing her back into the house and her captivity. And anyone who saw it happen would be on Evelyn's side.

For the moment there was nothing for it but patience.

It was soon after this that a subtle change came over Evelyn's attitude to Mrs. Gosse. All at once she seemed to have become very tired of looking after the old lady. She hardly spoke to her, there were no pretty tray-cloths on the trays and the meals that she brought up as often as not consisted of meat of some sort out of a tin and a lump of mashed potato that had certainly come out of a packet. And Evelyn's face seemed to have become all bony jaw and veiled, resentful eyes.

One day, just as she was leaving the room, Mrs. Gosse said on an impulse, "Evelyn dear, don't you think it's time I was going home?"

Evelyn paused in the doorway. "So you want to leave us," she said.

"It's just that I think I've imposed on you long enough," Mrs. Gosse answered.

"You can go home tomorrow, if you want to," Evelyn said.

Mrs. Gosse tried hard not to look startled. "Just whenever it's convenient for you, dear," she said.

"Only tell me one thing first." Evelyn's voice suddenly grated. "Let's stop pretending, both of us. Oliver and I want to know if you've left us anything in your will, or does it all go to Judith?"

"I don't think that's a very nice thing to talk about," Mrs. Gosse replied. "I'd sooner not discuss it."

"But we want to know where we are. It won't hurt you to tell us. We aren't as well off as we look. Oliver isn't as clever as he thinks about money."

Mrs. Gosse considered her answer carefully.

"Well, you know everything I have was left to me by Andrew," she said. "And Judith is his daughter. You're actually no relation of his at all. I wouldn't say you've any right to his money."

"Didn't he leave half of what he had to Judith and half to you, without any strings to it?" Evelyn said. "I remember him saying so once. You can do what you like with your share."

"And you think I ought to make a will, leaving it to you."

"I do. We're your only blood relations."

"And if I make this will, I can go home?"

"As soon as you like. If not . . ."

"Yes, if not?" Mrs. Gosse asked quietly.

Evelyn hesitated, then seemed to make up her mind.

"After all, why should you ever go home?" she said with a tight little smile. "Your friends are already beginning to forget you. When you first came here they were always ringing up to ask how you were, but it was quite easy to put them off, and now they just think you've settled down with us and they've stopped worrying about you. You could stay on here in this nice room for ever and ever and no one would ask any questions. And as I really find carrying trays up and down the stairs rather a tiring job, perhaps I might not bother with them quite as often as I do. And I might forget to change your library books. I don't mean, of course, that I'd ever do anything actually unkind, but you might find your life not quite as comfortable as it has been. And still no one would dream of interfering."

"But suppose I make a will of the kind you want," Mrs. Gosse said, "what's to stop me changing it as soon as I get home?"

"If you promised you wouldn't change it, you wouldn't," Evelyn said. "That's what you're like."

"Are you sure?"

"Oh yes, I'm sure. You'd never change it."

"No," Mrs. Gosse said thoughtfully, "perhaps not."

For, promise or not, once she had made that will she would be given no chance to change it. She would never get home. What she understood clearly as the result of this extremely upsetting conversation was that the Hassalls were going to see to it that she never left the house alive. Melodramatic as it sounded, that was the simple truth. It must be. No other explanation of their actions made sense. And she was in their hands, at their mercy.

After that day, as if she were already putting her threat into practise, Evelyn became more and more neglectful of Mrs. Gosse. Her food was often hardly eatable. She had to struggle to make her own bed. The room was left to grow dusty and the sheets were not changed. And as she became better able to walk about she found, not much to her surprise, that she was locked into her room. In a way she was glad to be left alone. She liked it better than those times when the Hassalls tried to make her discuss her will. But sometimes she sat and cried from sheer loneliness and fear and hopelessness. The thought of giving in to them, trusting that at least the manner of her end would be merciful, began to seem almost attractive.

Then one afternoon, when she was in the bathroom, a noise in her bedroom startled her. It sounded as if the window had just been opened and closed. Then distinctly she heard footsteps and someone began to sing thickly and hoarsely.

"'When they call the roll up yonder,
    When they call the roll up yonder,
    When they call the roll up yonder,
    I'll be there. . . .'"

A burglar?

A burglar who came in daylight and sang hymns? Hardly likely. Yet burglars seemed to do the oddest things nowadays. One was always reading about it. And perhaps this one might turn out to be a friend. Limping into the bedroom as fast as she could, she saw a small, stout, red-faced man busily cleaning her window.

The window-cleaner. The one intruder whom the Hassalls had forgotten to keep out. And luckily, just then, Evelyn was away from the house, doing the shopping.

"Oh, good day," Mrs. Gosse exclaimed excitedly. "What a beautiful day it is, isn't it?

For almost every conversation with a stranger should begin with a remark about the weather, shouldn't it? It always eased things. Besides, for the first time for some weeks, she had just noticed how brightly the sun was shining.

He took no notice.

"Good day," Mrs. Gosse repeated, louder.

He went on polishing and singing to himself.

She went closer to him and tapped him on the shoulder with a crutch.

He whirled, his hands coming up as if to defend himself. Then, seeing her, he gave a loose-lipped smile and said, "Oh, good afternoon, missus. Didn't know anyone was in. Mrs. Hassall always says, if I come when she's out, go ahead on my own, she'll pay me next time. Nice day, isn't it?"

Mrs. Gosse's heart sank. She could smell the beer on his breath. He was, she realised, both drunk and deaf.

She tested how deaf he was by raising her voice and repeating as loudly as she could, "It's a beautiful day."

He gave her a dubious stare, considered the situation, then said, as if he knew that it was a safe thing to say in almost any circumstances, "That's right." Then he returned to polishing the window.

Mrs. Gosse stumbled hastily to the table where her writing paper and envelopes were. She lowered herself into the chair there and began feverishly writing. Before she was half finished, the window-cleaner began to climb out of the window on to his ladder. She reached out with one of her crutches and jabbed him sharply. He turned with a look of hurt protest. She held up a finger, beckoning to him, and shouted, "Wait!"

He stayed where he was uncertainly while her ballpoint jabbed at the paper.

Under the address that she had scrawled at the top, she wrote, "Dear Mr. Deane, I am being kept here against my will. I am in fear of my life. Please come and rescue me. This is very urgent. Yours sincerely, Margery Gosse."

She folded the sheet of paper, slid it into an envelope and addressed it. She had an uneasy feeling that what she had written might sound merely insane. If she had had more time to think, she might have written more temperately. But the window-cleaner was looking as if he might decide to descend his ladder at any moment. Then she realised that she had no stamps. Taking fifty pence out of her handbag, she handed it to him with the letter, pointed at the corner where the stamp should have been and shouted, "Please! Please post it for me!"

At the sight of the fifty pence his face split open in a grin.

"Thank you, missus," he said. "Very good of you. Thank you."

"But please post the letter!" In her own ears her pleading voice sounded hopelessly thin and ineffectual.

"That's right," he said cheerfully, pocketed the money and holding the letter, disappeared.

Mrs. Gosse got up, lurched to the window and looked down after him.

She saw him reach the bottom of the ladder, look at the letter in his hand in a puzzled way as if he wondered how he had come by it, then crumple it into a ball and drop it on a flower-bed.

Mrs. Gosse tugged at the window to open it, to shout down to him to post the letter at all costs. But the catch of the window stuck and by the time that she had somehow managed to undo it, the man had moved on out of sight.

She collapsed into a chair. For a few minutes she gave in to helpless sobbing. The bitter disappointment after the few minutes of exalted hope left her feeling far more desperate than she had before. She felt more exhausted than she ever had in her life. A cloud of blackness settled on her mind. Utter despair enveloped her. Now there was nothing left for her, she knew, but the gamble that she had been thinking about recently. A most fearful gamble. The thought of it terrified her. For it was only too likely to fail. But if it did, did she really care? Might that not be better than letting things go on as they were now? All the same, but for the agonizing disappointment of having seen her letter crumpled and dropped on the earth, she would probably never have had the courage to act.

As it was, she sat still, thinking, for what seemed a very long time. She had never been a gambler by nature. She enjoyed her bridge, but never for more than twopence a hundred, and once, when she and Andrew had been in Monte Carlo, she had become very agitated when he had risked a mere twenty pounds at roulette. Yet here she was, thinking of risking all that she had. Literally all. Her life.

At last she got up, and staggering more than she usually did now, from nervousness and a kind of confusion, she went into the bathroom, took her sleeping-pills out of the cabinet and counted them. There were forty-seven in the bottle. And the lethal dose, she had been told some time, was around thirty. But when you were eighty-two, perhaps it would not take so many to kill you. How could you tell? You must just guess and hope for the best. Above all, you must not take too few. That would be useless. Counting out thirty, she flushed them down the drain. Then with shaking hands she filled a glass of water and set herself to swallowing all the pills that remained.

She was surprised at how calm she became while she was doing it. Walking back into her bedroom, she turned the cover of the bed down neatly, took off her shoes and lay down. While she was waiting for the drug to begin to affect her she found the words of the hymn that the window-cleaner had sung going round in her head. Dimly, they comforted her.

She was far gone by the time that Evelyn came in with her supper tray. Loud snoring noises came from the inert figure on the bed and the aged face on the pillow was paper-white. Evelyn stood still, staring, then shouted, "Oliver! Oliver, come at once!"

He came pounding up the stairs.

"Look!" Evelyn cried.

"Oh God, what's happened, what's she done?" he gasped.

Evelyn dumped the tray that she had been clutching on the table and shot into the bathroom. She came out with the empty bottle.

"It's her pills. She's taken the lot. What fools we've been, leaving them here! Why didn't we think she might do this?"

"How many were there?"

"Nearly fifty, I think."

"Then she hasn't a hope."

"What are we going to do? This isn't how we planned things. There'll be questions, a post mortem. . . . Oh, Lord, when I think of all the time I've spent on her—"

"Be quiet, let me think."

"We'd better get the doctor."

"Yes, yes, of course, that's unavoidable. But the question is, do we do it now, or—when it's over?"

"It had better be now," Evelyn said. "If she's going to die anyway, it's going to look better if we do everything we can to save her. It might even give us some sort of claim against the estate."

"You can forget that now. That damned woman Judith will get the lot. And suppose she comes round. Wouldn't it be better to wait? We can't have her talking."

"She'll never come round. Go and phone the doctor. We can tell him she was convinced she'd never walk properly again and that that had been depressing her. Go on."

"And you'd better do some cleaning up in here," Oliver said. "The place looks filthy. We've got to make it plain we've been doing everything we could for the woman. Hurry."

He went away along the passage to the telephone extension in the bedroom. Evelyn, giving the figure on the bed a look of the deepest malignancy, set about giving the room a rapid dusting.

Mrs. Gosse, in her deep coma, went on with her unconscious struggle for life, drawing one snorting breath after another into her labouring lungs. The effort of each breath seemed to use up more of her vitality than she could possibly afford. She looked far too wasted and fragile to survive till rescuers came.

It was morning when she recovered consciousness in the hospital. Through a fog, she became aware of people coming and going, of a bright young face under a starched cap bending over her, of voices nearby and of someone saying, "She'll do."

She could not think how it had come about. Her memory was a blank. But a sense of wonderful peace enveloped her. There was something beautiful about seeing human faces round her and the two rows of beds filled with other sick people in the long emergency ward. She smiled vaguely at a man who was standing by her bedside and murmured, "Are you from the police?"

"Of course not, I'm a doctor," he said. "And a lot of trouble you've given me. If you weren't as strong as a horse, we'd never have pulled you through. But we don't need the police just because you took a few too many of your pills, do we? That's all that happened, isn't it? You lost count. We don't need the police just because you were a little careless."

"The police," she said softly, as if it were a word that charmed her, then she drifted off into a normal sleep from which she did not wake for several hours.

When she woke, Evelyn Hassall, holding a bunch of lilac, was standing at the side of the bed.

Mrs. Gosse raised her head a little from the pillow and began to scream, "Nurse, nurse, nurse!"

Her mind was as clear as it had ever been.

"Sh, darling, don't, you'll disturb everyone," Evelyn said. She looked hollow-eyed, as if she had not slept during the past night, but she smiled sweetly.

"Nurse, nurse!" Mrs. Gosse shrieked.

The heads of the other patients in the ward turned towards her. A nurse came running.

"Now, now, what's this?" she said. "This is your niece, Mrs. Hassall. Don't you recognise her? She sat up all night while we worked on you and it was touch and go. She'll take you home again as soon as you're strong enough."

"Don't let her come near me!" Mrs. Gosse shouted so that everyone could hear. "She gave me that stuff to drink. She tried to kill me. I told her I was going to change my will because she and her husband were so unkind to me and she gave me all that poison in my tea before I could call my lawyer. My lawyer, Mr. Deane. I want to see him now. I want to see him at once because I mean to change my will immediately and leave everything to my stepdaughter, Judith."

"*Change* your will . . . ?" Evelyn began.

"Yes, yes, I'd left everything to you, you knew that," Mrs. Gosse answered furiously. "When Andrew and I made our wills he said to me he was providing for Judith himself and that what he was leaving me was mine absolutely and that I should leave it, if I wanted to, to my own kith and kin. So I left it all to you and you would have had it if you hadn't been too impatient. Trying to poison me, that's further than I thought even you would go, that's murder. Nurse, I want the police. I want to charge that wicked woman with trying to kill me."

"But I didn't know about your will. . . . You didn't say . . . And I didn't give you anything, you took it yourself!" Evelyn's eyes were wide and frightened in her pallid face. Her bony jaw trembled.

Suddenly she turned and went running out of the ward, dropping the lilac as she ran.

Mrs. Gosse gave a deep sigh. Settling herself more comfortably in the high, hard bed, she smiled up at the nurse.

"Of course, I knew there was something wrong with the tea as soon as I tasted it," she said. "But I thought perhaps the teapot hadn't been washed out properly. My niece is not as careful a housekeeper as she might be. But I didn't want to make a fuss. I never make a fuss if I can help it. And naturally I never thought of murder. But I'm afraid there's really no question of it. So now, dear, I'd really like to see someone from the police. After all, poisoners nearly always try again."

The nurse gazed at her with a look of shock on her face, then went hurrying away to consult the sister.

Perhaps because Mrs. Gosse was not wearing her false teeth, which were in a glass by her bedside, her gentle features looked more shrunken than usual, more hollow, so that her jawbone stood out, giving it almost as hard an outline as that of her niece Evelyn.